I0819545

THROUGH GATES OF GARNET AND GOLD

BY THE SAME AUTHOR

Deadlands: Boneyard
Dusk or Dark or Dawn or Day
Dying with Her Cheer Pants On
Laughter at the Academy
Letters to the Pumpkin King
Overwatch: Declassified: An Official History of Overwatch
The Proper Thing and Other Stories
What If: Wanda Maximoff and Peter Parker Were Siblings?
Velveteen vs. The Early Adventures

THE ALCHEMICAL JOURNEYS SERIES

Middlegame
Seasonal Fears
Tidal Creatures

THE WAYWARD CHILDREN SERIES

Every Heart a Doorway
Down Among the Sticks and Bones
Beneath the Sugar Sky
In an Absent Dream
Come Tumbling Down
Across the Green Grass Fields
Where the Drowned Girls Go
Lost in the Moment and Found
Mislaid in Parts Half-Known
Adrift in Currents Clean and Clear
Seanan McGuire's Wayward Children, Volumes 1–3 (boxed set)
Be Sure: Wayward Children, Books 1–3

THE OCTOBER DAYE SERIES

Rosemary and Rue
A Local Habitation
An Artificial Night
Late Eclipses
One Salt Sea
Ashes of Honor
Chimes at Midnight
The Winter Long
A Red-Rose Chain
Once Broken Faith
The Brightest Fell
Night and Silence
The Unkindest Tide
A Killing Frost
When Sorrows Come
Be the Serpent
Sleep No More
The Innocent Sleep
Silver and Lead

THE INCRYPTID SERIES

Discount Armageddon
Midnight Blue-Light Special
Half-Off Ragnarok

Pocket Apocalypse
Chaos Choreography
Magic for Nothing
Tricks for Free
That Ain't Witchcraft
Imaginary Numbers
Calculated Risks
Spelunking Through Hell
Backpacking Through Bedlam
Aftermarket Afterlife
Installment Immortality

THE INDEXING SERIES

Indexing
Indexing: Reflections

THE GHOST ROADS SERIES

Sparrow Hill Road
The Girl in the Green Silk Gown
Angel of the Overpass

AS A. DEBORAH BAKER

THE UP-AND-UNDER SERIES

Over the Woodward Wall
Along the Saltwise Sea
Into the Windwracked Wilds
Under the Smokestrewn Sky

AS MIRA GRANT

THE NEWSFLESH SERIES

Feed
Deadline
Blackout
Feedback
Rise: The Complete Newsflesh Collection (short stories)
The Rising: The Newsflesh Trilogy

THE PARASITOLOGY SERIES

Parasite
Symbiont
Chimera

Rolling in the Deep
Into the Drowning Deep

Overgrowth
Final Girls
Kingdom of Needle and Bone
In the Shadow of Spindrift House
Square^3
Unbreakable
Alien: Echo

THROUGH GATES OF GARNET AND GOLD

SEANAN McGUIRE

TOR PUBLISHING GROUP
NEW YORK

This is a work of fiction. All of the characters, organizations, and events portrayed in this novella are either products of the author's imagination or are used fictitiously.

THROUGH GATES OF GARNET AND GOLD

Interior illustrations by Rovina Cai

A Tordotcom Book
Published by Tom Doherty Associates / Tor Publishing Group
120 Broadway
New York, NY 10271

www.torpublishinggroup.com

EU Representative: Macmillan Publishers Ireland Ltd, 1st Floor, The Liffey Trust Centre, 117–126 Sheriff Street Upper, Dublin 1, DO1 YC43

The Library of Congress Cataloging-in-Publication Data is available upon request.

ISBN 978-1-250-33940-9 (hardcover)
ISBN 978-1-250-33941-6 (ebook)

First Edition: 2026

Printed in the United States of America

10 9 8 7 6 5 4 3 2 1

FOR NATALIE,

FOR DAYS AND DOORS TO COME

PART I

AN OPEN DOOR

THE PLACES WE GO

DOORS ARE MAGICAL THINGS. Always. It doesn't matter whether they connect two familiar, well-known rooms or two entirely undiscovered spaces: to travel from one distinct location into another simply by passing through a portal, whether bound in wood or carved from stone, is a magical act.

Doors are symbols of security. They can be closed; they can be locked; they can be used to keep the inside in and the outside out. A door means captivity, in one context, and freedom, in another. Like all forms of magic, they are constantly changing, transformed by surroundings and by circumstance.

Almost as long as there have been people, there have been doors. In the beginning, they were sheets of hanging leather or bundles of dried grasses, branches cut from plants with large, broad leaves. They offered privacy and transition, not security, but they were a beginning, and their creation changed every world that they began on. For doors were never the creation of a single world, never a close-kept secret or forbidden lore; doors were for everyone, and for everywhere.

Almost as soon as the first door was hung, the first Door opened from one world into another, hungry and questing for something that didn't have a name. No one knew about them in those days. Parents didn't yet tell their children stories about monsters under beds and lurking in the backs of closets, didn't yet have cause to fear the transition between one place and another. But the doors were built, and the Doors were open, and everything was changing.

The first Doors were clumsy predators, unpracticed, swinging open for unsuitable victims and sweeping them away on wild adventures that they could never have anticipated. The ones who survived most often returned to their homes with pockets full of parables and heads full of incredible, indescribable things. They spread stories and sciences from world to world, speaking with a child's innocence of the wonders they had seen on the other side of their journeys. The children who did not return were often seen as a reasonable payment for the glories that the Doors enabled.

Time went on. The Doors became more skilled in their hunting, more targeted with their lures. Fewer and fewer children returned to their worlds of origin, and for those they left behind, it was impossible to tell whether this was due to contentment or death. Stories began to spread, stories of wonderful, terrible temptations that would steal children from their homes and families, never to return.

As the stories spread, the targets of the Doors learned caution, learned to avoid an impossible temptation, and more often turned away from the fantastic. The flow of innovations and epiphanies from the other side slowed to a trickle, until the wonders from beyond the Doors could be dismissed as the imaginings of children, or the inspirations of a budding genius. A story stopped the stories, a true story which, of necessity, began to fade into fiction as the Doors became less common and less easily seen.

But the exchanges never truly stopped. The Doors might take more care in their manifestation than they had in the beginning, might select their targets with more precision, but they still appeared. They still stole, they still hunted, and nothing was going to change that, short of a massive upset in the nature of reality itself. Children still walked through doorways, slipped through missing boards in fences, climbed under strangely shaped archways formed of tree boughs and shadow, and disappeared.

And sometimes those children came back.

Came back to a world that no longer had the vocabulary to describe what had happened to them, that no longer knew how to respect the fact that sometimes time was a ribbon, and ribbons can be tangled, or snarled, or woven into knots; that would treat them as children after they had saved an entire world and become someone entirely different in the process. They came back for many reasons. They came back because their quests were ended, because they missed their homes and families, because they wanted to be children again, after all the wars were ended. Or they came back because they had stumbled during a moment of weakness, and fallen through a doorway only halfway seen.

"Be Sure" was the commandment of the Doors, their requirement for passage and their only coin. As long as their travelers were convinced of the rightness of their journey, it would continue smoothly and uninterrupted. Let that conviction waver for even a moment, however, and they might find themselves dumped back in the world of their origin, abandoned by the Doors, unable to return to the world they had come to consider home.

It was perhaps inevitable that one of those children, whose certainty had wavered, would eventually begin to gather the others, plucking them from situations they no longer understood, from families who saw their experiences as dreams and their desires as delusions, and bring them together to support one another in their grieving for the Doors. Eleanor West's

Home for Wayward Children was school and sanitarium combined, a place to recover from unimaginable wounds, and a place to relearn the world as it was after losing the world as it might have been. She took all who had returned from their journeys, voluntary or not, and who still wanted to remember the wonders they had seen.

Much like the Doors themselves, Eleanor's rules were simple and absolute:

No solicitation. No visitors.

No quests.

1 SCREAMS AGAINST SILENCE

SILENCE HELD SWAY OVER the Halls of the Dead. It extended from the pomegranate groves that welcomed all travelers, living or dead, all the way to the fields of asphodel beyond the palace proper. When it was broken—which was more rarely than most people would assume—it was quick to cover the cracks, restoring them to perfect quiet.

But despite the silence, and despite the name the place had chosen for itself, the Halls of the Dead were very much alive. The trees in the pomegranate groves put forth green leaves and new fruit, and they never bowed their heads to winter; instead, they were somehow caught in an endless cycle of growth and harvest, flowers budding even as the ripe pomegranates fell to the grass and scattered garnet seeds in all directions. If anything, they were more alive than their counterparts in the supposedly realer worlds from which their travelers came, and their fruits were tartly sweet in a way that left no need for augmentation or accessory. One of their pomegranates was a full meal unto itself, and could satisfy any hunger.

The flowers in the fields of asphodel were much the same. They blossomed and withered, only to be immediately replaced by fresh, sweet-scented buds, their petals forever straining to reach the sky. Their perfume could cure any mortal ill, heal any wound, and the physicians of a thousand worlds would kill for a single petal. The Halls of the Dead were bursting with so much life that it seemed they must split their seams, overflow their foundations, and pour through the Doors to every world that was.

Most damning in the eyes of the unfamiliar, however, were the living statues who attended on the Lord and Lady of the Dead—for make no mistake, all the life that filled the Halls did not cancel out the presence of the dead, who were a constant reminder that all life must one day end, and all flesh must one day decay. In the parts of the Halls most favored by the Lord and Lady, in the grounds where they walked together, the living statues stood.

They were the children of the Doors, the ones who had been lured to a place that masked its endless, teeming life in a shell of silence and serenity, and the Halls had given them the gift of stillness. Those who managed to make a home for themselves in the Halls did so by becoming so motionless that they appeared to have been carved from marble, assuming beautiful poses and holding them so absolutely that their very cells forgot the process of growing older. The living statues breathed perhaps once an hour, and this was twice as frequent as the beating of their hearts. When they ate, it was wafers of sugar slipped between their lips by attendants, or sponges soaked in pomegranate juice pressed to their mouths until the juice trickled down their throats without the need to swallow. When they slept, it was in elegant poses draped like lace around the bases of marble plinths, their arms and legs akimbo.

Some of the statues had been there for centuries, refining the art of their motionlessness. The Halls of the Dead had no real dangers, not the way some worlds did: no dragons to fight, no evil empires to bring low. What they had was time, and peace, and a place to be silent and still while you thought your way through all the troubles of your life. Their greatest cruelty was also their greatest kindness, for many, when they finished thinking their way through everything that needed to be considered, would find that the lives they had left behind were decades in the past, their names added to the rolls of those lost to the danger of the Doors.

Nancy had been in the Halls of the Dead for years. She could hold herself so exquisitely still that her blood slowed in her veins, her breath stopped in her throat, and only her mind was left to race ahead, thinking as quickly as it ever had. She was one of the Lord of the Dead's most beloved statues, for she bent herself into beautiful shapes whenever she was given the word to move, finding new ways to angle her chin, to lift her arms, until she looked like she truly *was* carved of flawless marble, created by some unknown artisan's hand.

She had no regrets. Even in the moments when her mind trended toward the melancholy and memories of the friends she'd left behind in her world of origin, she had no regrets. Her time before the Halls had been fast and frantic, filled with people who wanted things from her that she was ill-equipped to give. Here, she had the time to consider the world in more depth, to truly understand herself, and she treasured that. In time, she thought, she might tire of it, and seek to go back to where she'd come from. Everyone she'd ever known would be long dead of old age by that point, and she would still be herself, exactly as she was now.

Somehow that thought was exhilarating, rather than terrifying. They had been so sure that she was dreaming of death when she said she wanted to go home, when she'd been dreaming of living all along. Living the better part of forever, unmoving and unbroken. Perfect, forever.

She was standing on her daytime plinth, one foot kicked

back so that only her toes touched the marble, the other foot flat and stable, giving her a firm base to rest upon. She had her eyes tilted toward the heavens, her chin canted ever so slightly upward, and her arms were raised as if she were going to embrace some descending companion, holding them close and safe when finally they reached her. She had been in that position for six hours, and would hold it for another four before the bell rang for evening positions and she adjusted herself into the appropriate pose.

Nancy had been contemplating her evening position for the last several hours. The evening position was the shortest of the poses, held for barely four hours. Evening was the time to try new things, experimental things, without the fear of overbalancing that could attend on trying new positions during the day. Most daytime positions began as evening experiments, tested in the short term before they were adopted in the long term. Nancy was very proud of the fact that three of her evening poses had spread through the other statues, becoming common sights during the day.

She did wonder, sometimes, what her friends back at school would think if they could walk the Halls and see the living statues bending themselves into silent mirrors of their own posture. Would Sumi recognize herself in the position that looked like the statue was tensing to jump, weight precariously balanced on toe tips and counterweighted by the long, elegant stretch of the arms? Would Jack know her own stiff, unyielding posture when it was divorced from her clever hands and sharp tongue?

Would it matter if they did? She was never going to see them again. Practicing and releasing their echoes was the closest she could come, and that would have to be good enough, because she had no regrets. None at all. She was sure, and she

would remain sure, for as long as the pomegranates fell, as long as the asphodel bloomed.

It would have been natural, when a scream split the silent air and echoed through the Halls, to turn toward the sound. The statues were preternaturally still and composed, but they were still human—most of them, the ones who had been human to begin with—and they could still have their attention caught by the unexpected. From her position atop the plinth, Nancy saw several of the statues wince or tense, the sudden tightness of their jaws and shoulders betraying their weakness.

Only the older statues remained perfectly composed, as if the sound of screaming were no more unusual than the bell for change of posture. Nancy was proud to count herself among their number, even as she felt her heart beat twice, all out of sync with what she had worked so hard to achieve.

The screaming was followed by the sound of running footsteps, bare flesh against marble floors, and Nancy wondered who was running, whether they were worried about falling, whether they feared attracting the attention of the ghosts who haunted the Halls.

The statues hadn't come about to please the Lord and Lady's whims. The practice had evolved, beginning with the first child whose Door had led them to the Halls, as a form of camouflage and self-protection. Because the Halls of the Dead were filled with life and the living, yes, but their name came from their original occupants.

The dead. Ghosts from a hundred worlds flowed through the Doors to haunt the Halls. Some of them were at peace with what had happened to them, silent shades who went voluntarily to cloistered chambers full of endless darkness stolen from the end of all things. They manifested there as dancing motes of silver light, and lingered for a time, before they went back through the Doors to be reborn in some other world, some other time and place. Very few of those silver specks chose life on the same world twice in a row, and according to some of the oldest statues, if Nancy held her peace for long enough, she would see the same dancing motes over and over again, lost children who couldn't resist the call to adventure even long enough to rest. Those ghosts were harmless. They avoided contact with the living, and lingered only long enough to decide their next destinations.

But there were other ghosts. Angry ghosts who resented what had become of them, who thought they still belonged among the living—who hungered to return to what they had once been. They were mostly corralled, contained in special rooms carved not from void, but from the explosive birth of stars. In that crucible of birth and destruction, they could be reforged into something kinder, something less all-consuming.

When those ghosts ran free, the living died. They were attracted to life, heat . . . motion. All the things possessed by the living, all those things tamed and controlled by the statues, who had trained their bodies to mimic not death but inanimation.

The first statue had been a traveler who, when they saw their companions cut down and devoured by the dead, had frozen rather than fleeing for their own life. The dead had swept over and around that long-gone guest in the Halls of the Dead, leaving them unharmed, and the Lord and Lady had seen a way to protect the children who stumbled through the Doors and into their care. To protect them, and to honor their need for the quiet of the Halls, the pair taught the children who followed to embrace the stillness. They became sculptors of living statues, shaping and encouraging them, making their silence a barrier against the angry dead.

But now there was screaming in the Halls. It began with a single scream, rising to a terrible crescendo before it was cut abruptly off. There was a wet sound, a squelching horror, and the silence returned. Where it had been a warm, comfortable silence before, it was now echoing and terrible, like the pause before some great beast attacked.

Nancy reached for the stillness, forcing it through herself until her recalcitrant heart calmed and returned to its customary tempo, beating so slowly that any doctor would have declared her dead and gone. But she lived, as she had always lived, and she was not going to allow that condition to change, not if she had anything to say about it. She calmed herself, even as another scream rang out in the distance, and another after that, and another, until she could hear the rushing of an impossible wind in the pauses between the screaming, the susurration of a million ghosts rushing through unsealed chambers.

The statue across from her slipped.

Not much; not enough to fall. His heel simply turned out of true, and he stumbled. He recovered his composure quickly, but the damage had been done, and as sweat broke out on his temples, the rushing sound drew closer, skirling around him like the autumn wind. Like the autumn wind, it was tinted with frost and with decay. It wrapped tight, and Nancy watched, absolutely still, as it brushed against his skin.

He screamed. The rushing grew louder, and he came apart in the impossible wind, dissolving into a fine mist of skin, blood, and bone that stained the white chiton he'd been wearing in an instant, leaving the now-tattered garment to drop discarded to the floor. Surprisingly little of the red mist fell alongside it; most of the cloud that had been a living statue was carried away by the wind, whisked into the depths of the Halls.

Nancy watched the chiton fall, and did not move. Tears gathered in the corners of her eyes, and she did not move. One broke free and ran down her cheek, and for a moment, Nancy felt the phantom lick of the wind upon her own cheek. Then the sensation was gone, and the tear was falling, and she was alone.

Endlessly, absolutely alone.

2 WHEN WE'RE GONE

THE FIRST TIME NANCY had discovered the Door into the Halls of the Dead, it had been in the basement of the small suburban home she shared with her parents, tucked behind the washing machine, in a space that should have held only cobwebs and dust. She had pried it open with shaking fingers, sure that she was going to see nothing but the packed earth beneath the house, or possibly a long-forgotten root cellar—although that wouldn't explain how the door could appear out of nowhere, would it? Doors didn't simply snap into existence where they hadn't been the day before—and equally sure that if she didn't look, she would regret it forever.

But that door had opened on a grove of pomegranate trees, the grass lush around them and dotted with the jeweled husks of fallen fruit. Nancy had stepped through at once, and she'd been most of the way to the Halls proper before she heard the sound of a door closing far behind her.

When her conviction had later wavered, when she'd been less *sure* than her citizenship demanded, she had found herself stumbling through that same door, returned to the basement, returned to the silence beneath a house that had been feeling less like a home with every passing year, where she was expected to be a rainbow when what she wanted was to be elegant, and silent, and still. She had whirled around immediately, only to find the door was gone: there was only smooth concrete wall where it should have been.

She had started to scream at once, all her years of stillness falling away in the face of such impossible horror, and her parents had come thundering down the stairs, ready to confront the intruder in their basement. Only to discover their missing daughter in the middle of a meltdown, hysterical at first, then near-catatonic.

From there she had been sent off to what they called a boarding school but she knew was really just a glorified mental hospital for people who swore impossible things and refused to be swayed away from them. She'd been terrified when that happened, convinced that leaving the basement behind would mean she could never find her way home again.

But the school had turned out to be the best thing that could possibly have happened to her in a world of hot, fast creatures who moved like movement didn't matter, like it was something to be spent without thinking twice. At the school she had met other people who'd traveled the way she had, to worlds equally fantastic and impossible, and if none of them had truly appreciated the value of stillness, at least they'd been able to understand that it had mattered to *her*. At the school, she had found true friends and companions, and through the contrasts between her stories and theirs, she had been able to find her certainty. When the Door had opened again, this time in the basement beneath the school itself, she had been truly sure. She had been confident in her convictions, and she had never expected to come back.

No one else had been expecting her to return either, and her room had been given away with the start of the next term, becoming a comfortable home for a boy named Christopher Flores. He was stretched out on the bed with an anatomy textbook, idly twirling a bone flute between his fingers as he read. His eyes skimmed the pages with far more focus and fascination than most people would have expected from a boy of his age, barely able to look away from the illustrations.

He was so focused that he didn't even seem to notice when a door opened out of a flat stretch of wall and Nancy stepped through. She froze when she saw him, going utterly still. The doorknob slipped through her fingers, allowing the door to slide smoothly closed.

The soft click of the door closing caught his attention enough that he glanced up. Catching sight of Nancy, he yelped and scrambled further upright on the bed, heels digging at the covers in his quest for traction. Both book and flute went flying, leaving him empty-handed and staring at her.

This is what Christopher saw: she was tall, thin, and achingly pale, the kind of pale that skirted the line between "natural" and "spectral." She was wearing a knee-length white chitoniskos, belted at the waist with a braided cord of white, silver, and pomegranate crimson. Her hair, which was braided severely back, was white except for five black streaks, like the echo of fingers, and a red ribbon that matched her belt was clasped around her throat. She looked at him, and she didn't move, not even enough to look like she was breathing.

His own breath caught in his throat like a stone, Christopher pushed himself fully upright before carefully swinging his feet around to the floor and standing up. He took a step toward her, clearly unsure whether she was really there or just an apparition come to interrupt his reading.

"Nancy?" he said, and his voice was soft and careful, the kind of voice he might have used on a frightened animal.

After a pause so long that he began to question whether or not he had actually spoken, Nancy nodded. It was barely a twitch, but compared to her previous stillness, it was everything.

Christopher took another step forward. "Nancy! I didn't think— What are you doing— Why are you *here*?"

Nancy licked her lips—she had forgotten how *dry* the world could be, when you left the cool, comfortable Halls of the Dead—and answered, in a soft voice, "They were all dying. The Lady told me to run, and so I ran. I need help, Christopher, please."

Christopher listened with absolute solemnity, only taking another step when she was finished. "Of course we'll help you, Nancy. You're always welcome here."

This is what Nancy saw: a tall, skinny Latino boy with messy black hair and clear brown skin, wearing jeans, a flannel shirt, and socks, having been raised too well to wear shoes in the bed. His long-fingered hands were empty, which she knew even after her long absence was wrong, making him seem incomplete. Indeed, as soon as her gaze flicked to his hands, his cheeks reddened and he hurried to retrieve his bone flute from the floor where it had fallen, caressing it in silent fingerings of songs no living soul could hear.

"I . . . How long has it been for you?"

"Long enough," said Christopher, demurring slightly. "Hard to say with all the questing we're not supposed to have been doing all this time. How long's it been for you?"

"Years." More than a decade spent standing in frozen contemplation of the universe. But from her last trip to the Halls of the Dead, Nancy knew that a year in that world would generally correspond to a month or less in this one. Time didn't always run smoothly between realities, and that was before accounting for the way becoming a statue slowed and stopped a person's rate of aging.

"Years," he echoed. "And yet you came right back here. Were you that sure we'd all be waiting?" There was a challenge in his tone, a regretful twist that told her how hurt he was that she'd assumed none of them would find their Doors back to their own far-flung homes.

"No," said Nancy. "I wasn't sure at all, only sure the school would still be here. That Miss West would still be teaching—or if she wasn't, that she would have found a successor. Someone who could keep the fires burning. A place like this . . . it feels like forever. And besides, I didn't have a choice. This was where the door I took to get back to the Halls of the Dead opened, so this is where the door that let me leave would be. If I get to go home again after this, then that would change where any future doors back to this world open. It's in and out at the same place, no matter where I am in the Halls when I step through."

"Huh," he said. "Efficient, I guess, although—didn't you tell me some of the statues stay there for hundreds of years? What would happen if you came back, and the Door was underground, or in the foundations of a building, or underwater?"

"I guess I'd be crushed, or I'd drown," said Nancy.

"Brutal," said Christopher approvingly.

Nancy didn't say anything, just waited for his next question. It was strange, being back in a world where people said what they thought as soon as they thought it. In the Halls of the Dead, a thought had to linger for weeks or even months before it would be judged worthy of sharing, in hushed tones after the evening bell had rung and they had all sunk into their night poses to sleep and refresh themselves for the day to come.

People thought it must be lonely, to be a statue, but it wasn't, oh, it was so far from loneliness. There was connection when the lights were out and the silence broke into a hundred whispered conversations, everyone exchanging ideas that had matured enough to be worth loosing on the world. Nancy had found true friends in those nighttime whispers, people she would sorely miss if she never made it home again.

People she was no longer sure would survive long enough for her to return. It was fear for their well-being that put fire in her blood, that made it possible for her to move quickly enough for Christopher to see as she turned her head toward the stairs, looking to the door at their top, and asked, "Is Miss West still in charge?"

"Eleanor?" asked Christopher—needlessly, because they both knew who she meant. "She still pays the bills, yeah, but Kade manages most of the day-to-day operations anymore. She's been stepping back a lot the last year or so, and he's been stepping up."

Nancy blinked, eyes flicking over Christopher. "I thought Kade was your age?"

"He is," said Christopher. "I think he's like eight months older, but that doesn't really matter. No, we're the same age, and he shouldn't be doing any of this. He should be thinking about his future, what he wants to do, where he wants to go from here, but all his focus is on the school. It's like he can't let himself imagine anything else."

"That's not right."

Nancy turned to face the stairs, the most she had moved since arriving in the basement. Christopher blinked, resisting the urge to rub his eyes. Watching her move was like watching some strange stop-motion film: there was something *wrong* about it. She wasn't fluid or jerky, she was just . . . staccato, like she was made up of a million snapshots of motion rather than one smooth, continuous action.

It would fade with time. All the gifts of the Doors faded

with time, although some would always remain. Christopher's flute was a gift of the Doors, and he knew that if it ever lost its power, he would die in short order. Maybe Nancy's new way of moving was the same way. He didn't think so, though. Something about it felt more temporary than that, more like the afterimage left by a bright light shining in your eyes than an actual, material change.

"I should let her know what's happened," said Nancy. "I'm sorry to have interrupted you."

"Don't be," said Christopher. "I'm glad to see you, Nancy. I always liked you."

Not as much as Kade had liked her, and he wanted to be there to watch when the mild, often-taciturn older boy got his first look at the returned Nancy. It was fairly common knowledge among the older students that Kade had had a massive crush on Nancy by the time she'd vanished from the school—a crush that had been at least somewhat reciprocated.

He'd gotten over it, something that had to be easier to do when you knew that the girl of your dreams was off in another world with no intention of coming back. Christopher wouldn't know. The girl of *his* dreams was in another world, waiting for him to come home and join her forever. There had never been a moment's doubt in his mind that his Skeleton Girl would stay as faithful as he had, that she would know he'd find his way back to her. What was the point of crushes when you had perfection just on the other side of a Door?

The fact that once he went back to Mariposa, returning to *this* world would no longer be an option didn't really matter much to him. It was mostly other people who were bothered by the fact that once he found his Door, he intended to shed his skin as quickly as possible before he could be banished again. To them, cutting his flesh away in order to exist as a living skeleton was a strange sort of suicide. To him, the word "living" was all that mattered.

Still, for the moment, he followed Nancy up the stairs to the hallway, watching her strangely disjointed motions with a critical air. How long would it take for this world to sand her rough edges away? Had she moved like this the first time she'd returned, or was this a function of how much longer she'd been gone this time, how much more practice she'd had at holding herself so still that even age couldn't catch her?

And would having the answers change anything?

Nancy reached the door at the top of the stairs, opened it, and stepped through, pausing to wait for Christopher to catch up with her. He did, smiling reassuringly as he eased the door to what was now his bedroom closed again.

He had a feeling the rule against quests was about to be broken once again.

3 SHADOWS OF THE UNKNOWN

MUCH LIKE NANCY, ELEANOR WEST was older than she looked. Unlike Nancy, she looked very old indeed. Her skin was deeply seamed with wrinkles, and her curly white hair had taken on that baby-fine cottony quality that came only with great age. She wore it cut short enough that it formed a fluffy corona around her head, seeming to almost glow in the multicolored light from the stained-glass windows in her office. They were a riot of carnival shades, patterned with chaotic jigsaw collections of shapes, like the webs spun by drunken spiders. The curtains, which were never drawn, were mere gossamer panels, intensifying the spider comparison.

The light did nothing to dim the screaming rainbow of her sweater, or the clashing paisley pattern of her velvet pants. She was seated behind her desk, shuffling papers into a pile and staring dreamily off into space. She did that frequently these days; sometimes hours could pass with the same pile of papers in her hands, getting endlessly more and more out of order as she shuffled them together again and again.

The dreamy expression left her eyes in an instant when someone knocked on her door, replaced by a sharp, canny look that belied her attempts to come across as a kindly but fading grandmother.

"Enter," she called.

The door creaked open, wide enough to admit the dark-haired head of one of her long-term students. "Do you have a moment?" asked Christopher.

"For you, my boy, I have a minute, which is a monument of moments," said Eleanor brightly, and grinned at him. Mariposa was a surprisingly Logical world, far removed from her own travels, but he had been with her for long enough that she had become deeply fond of the boy. Part of her felt that any world where skeletons could walk and talk and operate an independent government was nonsensical enough to have been put on her side of the Compass, but her nephew insisted that it was a Logic world, and anymore, she trusted him more with the world alignments than she trusted herself.

"It's not just me," said Christopher, and pushed the door open wider, stepping into the office. He kept the door open behind him, and a familiar stranger stepped into the doorway. Eleanor gasped, putting her hands over her mouth, tears welling in her eyes as she stared at her first true success story, her long-lamented, much-missed impossible girl.

"Nancy?" she whispered.

"Hi, Miss West," said Nancy. She raised one hand and offered a small, reserved wave.

Eleanor stood so fast that she knocked her desk chair over. It fell with a heavy thud, the impact knocking several small objects off the nearby shelves. Eleanor didn't appear to notice. She was too busy staring at the girl in the doorway, devouring her with her eyes.

"I thought . . ." she said. "I thought you were *gone*. Gone forever and for always, back to the ghosts and the green."

"I was," said Nancy, before her face crumpled and she began to cry.

Like almost everything else she did, she wept without

moving or making a sound. Tears ran down her cheeks and dripped from her chin, snot dripped from her nose, and her cheeks grew red with grieving, but her shoulders didn't shake and she didn't so much as blink away the tears, only let them fall in their own time, pulled down by gravity. It was unnerving, to watch such clear, static distress.

Eleanor came around her desk, moving to put her hand on Nancy's shoulder. When Nancy didn't shrug her hand off, she gathered the girl into a hug, letting Nancy's tears soak into the fabric of her sweater.

"It's all right, my precious girl," she said, keeping her tone soothing. "It's all right. The wind blows west in winter and east in the dawning spring, and both are bright as the other, both are equally desired. We can mourn the winter when the thaw comes, but without it, the spring will not return. It's all right to grieve. It's all right to mourn what's missing. Spill your sorrows on the ground, and let the joy flow home."

Nancy cried and cried, her head gradually falling to the side to rest on Eleanor's shoulder, and Christopher watched awkwardly, clearly feeling like he was intruding, just as clearly unable to move away.

Finally, Nancy's tears began to taper off. Eleanor looked to Christopher, gesturing for him to come closer. When he hesitantly did, she reached out and touched his arm.

"There's a box of tissues on my desk," she said. "Be a love and get them for me, would you? I think Nancy would like to wipe her eyes."

Nancy would clearly like to do more than that. Snot was running down her upper lip, and the tears on her cheeks were so plentiful that she looked almost like she'd been putting her face into a tub of water. There would have been roughly the same amount of dry skin.

Christopher hurried to get the tissues, bringing them back to Eleanor and stepping back again, shifting his weight from one foot to the other as he looked between the two women. "I think I ought to— I'm going to go get Kade, all right?"

"No," said Eleanor, with surprising sharpness. "You're not. I know you all think me too dazed by the process of living to operate my own school, but my mind's still as sharp as ever it was, more's the pity, and I'm done sitting back and letting other people handle my troubles while I'm still here to take responsibility for them. I might have thought I could invite the loss of my wits like an honored guest if I just tried hard enough, but I can't, and I'm not willing to wait any longer. It was my waiting that let Seraphina's heart fester like a rotted sore, and now I fear she's too far gone to ever be healed."

Nancy sniffled before asking, voice thick from weeping, "Seraphina? The pretty girl? She's still here?"

"As if there's anywhere else she could go, when she's so lovely she could stop the hearts of the unprepared in their chests and leave them downed for dead," said Eleanor. "She'll be here until she finds a way to hide herself away or finds a Door back to the land that cast her out, and I'm not sure which is more likely. It seems most like she'll be here forever. Maybe she can join the teaching staff."

Christopher looked horrified at the very idea. "She can't be trusted around the other students," he said. "She still pushes people around when she wants to get her way, even after she promised you she was done with that sort of thing."

"Promises don't make pearls out of pudding," said Eleanor almost serenely. "She can swear to anything she wants, won't change her nature."

Nancy looked to Christopher. "I've missed a lot, haven't I?"

"You have," he said. "You remember Sumi's daughter?"

Nancy nodded very slightly.

"Well, we found Sumi's heart in Confection, right where we hoped it would be. Faced her Queen of Cakes, met the Baker—sort of Confection's god, the person who bakes the whole world and puts it together so it can keep on turning. She was very sweet. I expect she'll wind up here someday, but she made us promise not to go looking for her, because time in Confection isn't exactly like time is here, and by her count she would still be a child in this world, right now. If we found her, we might cut her off from ever going through her Door, and then she wouldn't be there to bake Sumi a new body. I don't like time travel. It makes my head hurt, and I think we should leave it alone as much as we can manage."

Nancy seized on what sounded like the only important part of that story: "Sumi's alive?"

Christopher nodded with far more vigor than Nancy had managed thus far. "Sumi's alive and here at the school, and she's going to be absolutely thrilled to see you. Probably almost as thrilled as Kade is. Oh, he's going to be *beside* himself when he finds out you're back."

"Really?" asked Nancy, voice soft.

"Really," said Christopher. "Let's see . . . Sumi's back. Nadya stayed behind in the Halls of the Dead, so you know that. A bunch of us went to the Moors to help Jack, and Cora had a little run-in with the Drowned Gods. It messed her head up pretty bad, and she transferred to another school for a little while, to deal with it. Then she came back, and we helped a girl named Antsy get home so she could help the magpies who watch over all the Doors. And Cora found a Door back to the Trenches a couple of months ago. She's gone now. I hope she's happy."

His voice turned wistful at the end, perhaps remembering

that his own Door was still waiting, perhaps missing absent friends. It was difficult to say. "I hope they're all happy," he said.

Nancy reached out, still moving with that strange stop-motion effect, and put her hand gently on his arm. "If they weren't happy, they wouldn't be sure enough to stay," she said.

He looked up, meeting her eyes. "Does that mean you weren't sure anymore?"

Nancy sighed, and the sound was a wind blowing through a graveyard, threading its way between the headstones. "I was happy, until my friends started dying," she said. "I know it sounds impossible to people who don't dream about stillness the way I do, but I was happy. I learned how to hold so still that even time lost sight of me, and how to dream so hard that hours would pass between blinks, and I was happy. I've never been happier in my entire life. I could have stayed there forever. I was going to stay there forever. I was going to stand perfectly still, until the world forgot I had ever existed, and I was going to *stay* happy."

"So what happened?" asked Christopher. Eleanor, perhaps assuming that Nancy would be more inclined to answer someone her own age—or close to it—let go and stepped back, leaving them to face each other with no one else between them.

"I . . . It wasn't wanting to be dead that made us hold still. If anything, it was the opposite," said Nancy. "The dead are never still, not in their own halls. They dance and they fly and they flit from place to place like they're afraid of being pinned down to flesh again, because they are. Either they're afraid of rebirth, or they're afraid of letting go of what they were before they came to us. To be dead is to be in constant motion."

Christopher, thinking of the dancing skeletons of Mariposa, nodded.

"We hold still because the dead are *hungry*," she continued. "If they realize that we're alive, they'll devour us. That used to happen in the Halls, before the first statues realized that if they just stopped, they would be spared. So we learn the traditions of stillness and silence from the ones who have survived thus far, and the doors only seek out the ones who need that chance to pause and think for a little while, and the circle holds. I was going to stay, I was *so sure*."

"That's not an answer to my question," said Christopher.

"I'm getting there!" said Nancy, sounding frustrated. "You get out of practice actually answering questions when all you have to do is look at the inside of your own thoughts and stack your words up in beautiful towers that will never see the sun. I'm trying to answer, but you have to let me get there the way I know how to get there. You have to let me take the path that I can see."

"Sorry," said Christopher, not entirely mollified.

"It's all right," said Nancy. "It's been a while since I actually tried to have a conversation. I was sure, and then . . . things changed. Something upset the dead, enough that they tore through the Halls, and they devoured every statue who was anything less than perfect. They ripped my friends apart in front of me, and I couldn't react, couldn't even close my eyes or turn away, or they would have had me too. The Lady of the Dead came to me after the ghosts passed. She told me it wasn't safe anymore. She told me she couldn't protect me. And then she told me that if I stayed, I would probably die like all the others."

Nancy took a deep breath. "I didn't want to die. I *don't* want to die. I don't want my friends to die. If I can be sure enough to find another door to the Halls of the Dead, please. Please, I need someone to help me save them before it's too late. I know your students aren't supposed to leave campus during the week, but please, Miss West. Please, let us go and save the Halls of the Dead."

Eleanor blinked. Then she sighed, heavy as a woolen blanket, and said, "I suppose you'd best go fetch Kade after all. It sounds like you children are going on another quest."

4 WHERE SHADOWS CREEP . . .

FINDING THE OTHER STUDENTS outside of class time was often something easier said than done. Christopher left Nancy and Eleanor in the office, promising a swift return, and ran off down the hall, trying to decide which way to go first. Kade was almost certainly in the attic, at the very top of the school, but the attic meant stairs and furthermore, finding Kade would mean going back to the office, because there was no way he'd be willing to put off helping Nancy while they searched the house for Sumi.

Sumi could be virtually anywhere. She could be in the music room, playing nonsensical cover songs on her violin; she could be in the turtle pond, trying to squeeze the turtles into dresses scavenged from dolls abandoned by departed students; she could even be in her room, staring at the ceiling and trying to interpret the shadows in the plaster the way some people would interpret clouds. Her flightiness was her most frustrating attribute at times like this.

In the end, Christopher sighed heavily and turned toward the attic stairs. They could always find Sumi later, after they had the beginnings of a plan.

Eleanor West's Home for Wayward Children was located in a rambling old house that had belonged to her family for generations, and had been expanded upon and added to for just as long. Most of the additions had taken place since Eleanor took ownership of the property, and while they followed the necessary limits for safety's sake—no building code violations here—that was about as far as it went, where logic was concerned. Doors were equally likely to lead to the outside, another room, or a blank expanse of wall; windows opened between rooms. Staircases bristled off unexpected places, and led to equally unexpected rooms.

Only the Nonsense children seemed to be able to follow the strange rhythms of the house with anything resembling consistency; the ones who'd traveled to worlds where mushrooms talked and gravity sometimes turned itself off for the amusement of the sunbeams themselves. Those students had spent so much time removed from the land of logic and reliability that they no longer batted an eye at the strangeness of a house that didn't rearrange itself, just followed unpredictable rules.

So Christopher was already at a disadvantage when it came to locating Sumi, who could move through the house with effortless ease. He pulled himself up the stairs to the attic, trying to tamp down his frustration, and rapped his knuckles against the wood. There was a thudding sound from the other side, accompanied by a slithering crash that could only be a stack of books falling to the floor, and then Kade was opening the door, disheveled but dressed, hair in his eyes as he peered at Christopher.

"What's on fire?" he asked, Oklahoma drawl clipped tight by the question.

Christopher shook his head. "Nothing," he said. "Nothing is on fire, or underwater, or impacted by any other form of natural disaster. I just need you to come and find Sumi with me."

"Sumi? Why?"

Christopher shrugged. "I think your aunt's about to send us on another quest."

"Quests are against the rules," said Kade. "Aunt Eleanor doesn't *send* us on quests, she just sighs and doesn't stop us when the quests come along."

"This one's different," said Christopher. "Can you help me find Sumi?"

Kade fixed him with a stern eye, frowning ever so slightly. "You're sure you want her?"

"I'm sure she'd skin me alive if I left her out of this one, and she always finds a way to involve herself whether we want her or not; let's see how different things are when she's invited from the very start."

Christopher leaned forward, grabbing the other boy by the wrist. "Come on, Kade," he said. "You've been locked in your attic since Cora left, even though you knew it was what she wanted. You need to come out, and get back into the rhythm of things here. How else are you going to take over running this place?"

"What if I don't want to take over?" asked Kade, twisting his wrist out of Christopher's grasp and stepping back. "What if I want to do something else with my life?"

"Then you can do something else with your life, but whatever that is, you can't do it from your attic."

Kade sighed, rolling his eyes theatrically as he began to unbutton and rebutton his vest, getting it on straight. Christopher was privately glad to see that, even if he wasn't telling Kade the reason for their impending quest just yet; Kade would have *killed* him if Christopher had let Nancy see him for the first time since she went back to the Halls of the Dead with his vest buttoned wrong.

"Rake a brush through your hair," he said abruptly.

Kade fixed him with a dubious look. "Why?"

"Your aunt will kill me if I bring you in front of her with

messy hair." Christopher wanted to snatch the words back as soon as they were out, but couldn't. The lie hung between them, too large and blatant to be believable, and they both considered it for a beat so long that Christopher began to wonder whether it would hurt when Kade pushed him down the stairs.

To his surprise, Kade only shrugged and said, "All right," ducking back into the attic for a long minute. When he emerged again, his hair was brushed, his vest was buttoned, and he looked more himself than he had in months.

"Come on," said Christopher, tasting candy-sweet relief. "Let's find Sumi."

KADE'S METHOD FOR FINDING Sumi was simultaneously practical and ridiculous, much like Sumi herself, which might have been part of why it worked so well. "Think of all the places Sumi might be," he said to Christopher. "Then dismiss them, and think of all the places Sumi *isn't*. That's our list. That's how we're going to find her."

With that paradoxical instruction in mind, the pair of them left the attic, descending first to the library, where Sumi wasn't, and then to the laundry room, where Sumi wasn't either, and finally to the conservatory behind the main house, which Talia had converted into a massive incubator for rack upon rack of cocoons. They dangled, green and brown and yellow, some twitching as the moths within them struggled to be born, and moths fluttered through the glassed-in air, wings catching the slight currents that happened even inside a confined room.

Talia released the day's moths each night, standing outside next to a spherical light designed to mimic the moon, and if she cried, no one who attended her nightly releases said anything about it, to her or to each other. The moths brought her peace, if not enough to make a difference, and at Eleanor West's school, people had long since learned not to question what brought people peace.

Sumi was there. She was stretched out flat on her back atop a decaying log that Talia had scavenged from somewhere in the nearby forest, her bare shoulders pressed into the moss and several large moths perched upon her face, their massive wings opening and closing in a slow rhythm, slow as a heartbeat, slow as a breath. Talia was nearby at one of her cocoon racks, misting them down with a spray bottle and watching as they twitched.

She glanced around when Kade and Christopher came inside, one eyebrow rising, and didn't say anything. She knew they weren't there for her.

As for Kade, he did manage a polite smile for Talia, along with a nod to acknowledge that he understood they were trespassing in her territory. This was her place, her kingdom of moths and silent wings, and only the invited were meant to walk here. Which somehow included Sumi. She was rude, crass, and loud, never having a thought she didn't think deserved to be voiced, but somehow, that endeared her to the rest of the students, rather than driving them away. Eleanor laughed whenever someone mentioned it.

"An open door is a blessing of nonsense," she would say if pressed, and then wave the whole topic off like it was an inconvenience she no longer wanted to deal with.

Kade kept walking until he was at the end of Sumi's log. Christopher followed. "Sumi," he said. She didn't respond, only remained still beneath her cloak of moths. "*Sumi*," Kade repeated, louder. "You need to pay attention to me now."

"Does she?" asked Talia. "You're not one of her teachers, and she's been here all afternoon—whatever mischief you're here to accuse her of, she didn't do it. She can't have done it."

Kade scoffed. "If she'd done it, we'd never know. Sumi's too good at what she does to get caught out that easy. Now come on, Sumi. Christopher's been looking all over the school for you. Says he's got a line on a quest that might want us in it."

Sumi sat up immediately, sending moths flying in all directions. "Why didn't you say so?" she asked, swinging her legs over to the ground and standing. "It's been boring as early morning since I got back here, and I'm ready to do something ill-advised and dangerous."

Talia put down her mister, moving closer to the group.

"We don't know that it's going to be ill-advised," said Christopher. "Dangerous seems pretty likely, from what I know so far, but I think this might be something a little lower on the peril scale than following the mad scientist through a door made of lightning to a world where the moon can have opinions about whether or not it ought to eat you."

"Danger is as danger does," said Sumi philosophically. She plucked a moth out of her hair, where it had taken an excessive interest in one of her genuine gumdrop barrettes, sticking around to taste the sugar after its fellows fled. "Shall we go consider questing?"

"I'm coming," said Talia abruptly. The trio turned to look at her, blinking quizzically. She looked back, jaw set in a stubborn line.

Talia wasn't a tall girl, being only a few inches taller than Sumi. She wasn't a skinny girl, but wasn't a fat girl either, existing in that awkward in-between space where it was difficult to find trousers that would fit her without going to the plus-size catalogs, and half of those were too large, sliding right off of her hips. She had the tawny skin and straight black hair she'd inherited from her Chinese mother, and the Canadian accent she'd been raised to while living with her European father. Really, the most remarkable thing about her was how intensely stubborn she could be when she got her teeth into something. They'd all witnessed it, usually during evening therapy sessions, where she'd continued to cheerfully talk over any teachers who tried to interrupt her during her recitation of the Great Song.

Her friendship with Sumi wasn't remarkable. Everyone had a friendship with Sumi of one shape or another, even Angela, who generally reserved all her friendliness and good behavior for Seraphina. Talia was quiet and reserved, still grieving the loss of her Door, but she smiled for Sumi, and the smiling seemed to do her good.

It didn't help with the stubbornness, of course, but even Sumi couldn't work miracles.

Kade looked dubiously at Talia. "You don't know what this is all about, what we might be agreeing to do, why it's even happening. Why would you volunteer?"

"I want to go home," she said flatly. "Everyone knows that the people who go on quests with you are the ones who get to go home. I wasn't here until after they were gone, but people have told me about the Wolcott twins, and how they kicked off the questing. You went to find Sumi, and Nadya didn't come back. You went to that other school and we got new students, but some of the people you freed didn't make it here because they found their Doors. You helped Nancy get home, and Cora got to leave right after. Quests change the probabilities. They tell the Doors we're sure. Well, I'm sure, and I need to get home before the text runs out. I'm supposed to be writing the next verses to the Great Song, and I can't do that from here. I'm coming with you."

"Better not argue, Kade-unmade," said Sumi. "Better get going. If there's a quest for questing, we need to get it started or you wouldn't be here now. That's the way with questing."

Kade looked between the two girls and sighed heavily. "Fine," he said. "I don't even know what this is all about, and maybe this stupid, but fine. It's not my job to keep you from shoving your arm into the quest. Let's go."

Together, the four of them left the warm air of the conservatory, leaving all the moths in view behind.

5 IN DOORLESS CHAMBERS

CHRISTOPHER TOOK THE LEAD as they were approaching Eleanor's office, subtly working his way up to the front of their little formation and then continuing as if this was nothing remotely unusual, as if he always tried to replace Kade as the leader of their strange outings. When he reached the door, he motioned for the others to stay where they were for a moment, then stepped into the office.

"I found them," he said. "Are you sure you just want to bring them in here, no warning?"

"You didn't warn them?" asked Nancy.

Christopher shook his head. "I thought that should be your decision."

"Ghostie-girl!" squealed Sumi behind him, launching herself into the room on a collision course with Nancy. She impacted with the taller woman, arms wrapping tight around her waist as she lifted her off her feet and spun her around. Nancy's natural stiffness aided with this process; she didn't bend or yield as she was hoisted and spun, only stared at Sumi, expression caught between fondness and surprise.

Christopher stood in the doorway, gawping, as Eleanor walked over and patted him on the shoulder. "If you wanted to make a grand presentation, you shouldn't have recruited a Nonsense girl," she said, affectionately. "May as well get Kade in here."

She stepped into the hall, only blinking once when she

saw Talia standing behind Kade. There was a green-and-silver moth perched on the girl's hair, where she had yet to notice it, and the sight drew a smile from Eleanor's lips, even as she stepped to the side, gesturing for them to go into the office.

"My darling boy, there's someone here who wants to see you," she said, turning that smile on Kade. It warmed and softened at the same time, looking at him. He bore such a strong resemblance to some of her childhood cousins, the West blood showing through, as it always seemed to do. They were called to travel, the children of her bloodline, and the only surprise when she'd heard from her niece that Kade had disappeared had been that he wasn't in the Nonsense world that stole so many of them away from home.

She would have known at once if he had passed beyond the gates of wonder and wilting. Even after all this time, she always knew.

Kade walked slowly to the office door, and Talia walked equally slowly behind him, watching him the whole way. For all her stated willingness to force her way onto this quest, she still seemed to have a sense of self-preservation, and was perfectly willing to let Kade be the first into the line of fire.

When he reached the door he stopped, putting his hands over his mouth and simply staring for several long, terrible seconds. Finally, he lowered them and asked, in a voice that was higher and squeakier than his norm, like it belonged to someone much younger, "Nancy?"

Nancy looked away from her solemn contemplation of Sumi, the other girl's face still held between her hands, like it was a rare bird that might fly away if she didn't hold it gently. Her eyes lit up, more quickly than was seemly for a living statue, and she turned fully around, beaming. "Kade!" she said gleefully. "Oh, I was *so* glad to hear that you were still here. Not because I want you to be trapped here or anything, just because I *missed* you."

She rushed across the office, which for Nancy meant moving at almost the speed of a normal person. She still had that jittery stop-motion look when she moved, and Christopher was pleased to see it stop Sumi dead in her place, eyes going wide and round with awed surprise.

"How are you *doing* that, ghostie-girl?" she asked. "Are you not a people anymore?"

"Sumiko!" said Eleanor, sounding scandalized. "You can't ask your friends if they're still people, it's cruel."

"I am a people," said Nancy, pausing just before she reached Kade, who was glaring at Sumi like she had just betrayed him beyond all forgiveness. "I'm just a people who's wired a little differently right now, that's all. I've been a statue for years. I need to relearn how to move."

Then she turned back to Kade, expression melting into a smile. "I missed you," she murmured, and put her arms around his shoulders, and held him close. He responded to her embrace by closing his own arms around her waist and holding her as tightly as he could without the risk of hurting her.

Several seconds ticked by in silence before Talia said, "I was promised a quest. This doesn't look like a quest. Who's that?"

Kade finally loosened his grasp on Nancy, pushing her out to arm's length so he could look at her as he answered Talia's question. "This is Nancy Whitman. She used to be a student here."

"Technically she still is," said Eleanor. "She never graduated, and I never took her off our roster. Her parents think she ran away again, and since they were wrong about her running away in the first place, I've never gone out of my way to correct them."

"Oh," said Talia, taking in Nancy's odd clothing and perfect posture. "Is she the quest?"

"I suppose I am," said Nancy, still looking at Kade like she thought he might disappear if she took her eyes away.

"Well, this is all very exciting," said Eleanor, clapping her hands together. "Who wants lunch?"

IT WAS EARLY AFTERNOON—too late for lunch, too early for tea—but the kitchen was always open, and the leftovers from the day's lunch buffet were still fresh in their plastic containers, all but begging to be eaten. Eleanor and Christopher began their food preparation for the group with gusto. It probably helped that all of them had actually *had* lunch already that day, except for Nancy, whose metabolism was so slow that she could have skipped a whole week's worth of meals without feeling hunger gnawing at her ribs. But creature of nonsense or not, Eleanor was well aware of how food and drink could act as social lubrication, opening the necessary space for difficult things to be exhumed.

So they set a table for six, with tea and delicate sandwiches for Eleanor, a heartier ham-and-cheese sandwich for Christopher, a crystal flute of pomegranate juice for Nancy, and a bowl of candy for Sumi. When it came to Talia, she hesitated.

"I'm sorry, dear," she said, after the silence had stretched out long enough to become awkward. "I'm afraid I don't know your specific dietary needs by heart just yet."

Children who had traveled to other worlds often came back with different needs than their counterparts who had remained safely home. It was something about the passage, about adjusting to the realities of life in another world entirely. Talia met Eleanor's earnest, hopeful eyes and visibly decided to take the statement at face value, not to be insulted by Eleanor's apparent disinterest in her specific situation.

"White rice and mulberry jam would be lovely, thank you," she said. "With soy sauce and chopsticks, if you please."

"Nice," said Sumi, approvingly. "A little salty and sweet to set the mood, huh? I like putting soy sauce on licorice sticks sometimes. It makes a flavor like nothing else in the whole world."

"That flavor is 'bad,'" said Christopher, deadpan, and Sumi crowed laughter.

Nancy leaned back in her seat, smiling slightly as she listened to the unfolding chaos.

"Very well, my dear," said Eleanor, and returned to the kitchen to get Talia's meal. When she returned, she brought a plate of barbecued chicken and corn bread for Kade, setting it down in front of him as she took her own seat. "Does everyone have something to eat?"

"You know we do, Auntie," said Kade. "Thank you. Now let's hear about this quest."

Nancy looked to Christopher, raising her eyebrows in a silent plea.

"She doesn't want to recap," he said, turning to face the newcomers. "So I'll summarize, and she'll correct me if I get anything wrong. All right, Nancy?"

"All right," she said.

"She's been in the Halls of the Dead, playing statue—"

"Wait," interrupted Talia. "She's dead?"

"No," said Christopher. "She's very much alive, like all the statues in the Halls of the Dead. I guess when your whole world is dead people, you start importing live ones to supplement the home décor. Nancy never died, she just went where all the dead people were. Same as I did, same as Emily did, same as Jack and Jill did. There are lots of Doors to places that seem creepy when they're not for you."

Talia nodded, looking slightly abashed. "All right," she said. "Continue."

"Thanks for the permission," said Christopher. "Anyway, Nancy was playing statue in the Halls of the Dead, and had been since she left here. But time doesn't work the same in that world as it does here, so for her, it's been years. She's very good at standing still as a consequence of all that time spent doing it, and she was going to keep doing it forever, but something pissed off the ghosts that haunt the Halls of the Dead—the *actual* dead people—and they started attacking the statues. So Nancy got the hell out of there and came here, because we might be able to help her save her friends. That sound about right, Nancy?"

"It's not perfect, but it's close," said Nancy. "The ghosts are attacking the living statues, and they're killing us. I need people to come with me to the Halls of the Dead, so we can save them."

"How are we planning on getting there?" asked Kade.

"You did it once before," said Nancy.

"We had Rini with us then, and she had a bracelet made of magic sugar beads that let her open up Doors so she could accomplish her own quest. We don't have one of those now."

"Oh," said Nancy, wilting slightly. "Well, I only left because I was told to go and find help. I'm still sure of where I belong, where I want to be, and it's not here." She didn't appear to notice the way Kade winced at her words, like they had been aimed directly at him. She just looked down at her glass of pomegranate juice, gently twisting the stem back and forth.

Sumi saw that and tensed. If Nancy was fidgeting, even in such a small, dismissible way, she was even more distraught than she appeared. Not that the ghostie-girl looked overly distraught from the outside, but Sumi knew her better than most people did. Sumi could tell.

"I think I can find a Door home if I stand still long enough and really focus," said Nancy. "I'm ready to try."

"So the quest depends on someone being able to summon a Door just by wanting it hard enough?" asked Talia. She slumped back in her chair. "If that worked, we'd all be out of here."

"Not necessarily," said Sumi. "While I was with Antsy in the Store, I learned a lot about how the Doors work. They don't hone in on wanting. Everyone *wants*, kids especially. A child is a vessel for wanting—and snot. Lots of snot in your average kid. Anyway, wanting isn't the point. It's the certainty. The absolute conviction that you're willing to give up everything you know, everything you have, if you can just go somewhere that you'll be understood. Most people don't have that, or if they do, they don't have it for very long."

"Being absolutely sure is hard on the human heart," said Eleanor. "We're creatures of contradiction, and that's how we survive. We need a little nonsense in us to cut all the routine away. And nonsense is like acid for certainty."

"That's easy for you to say," snapped Talia. "You know where your Door is. You could go back any time you wanted."

Eleanor didn't respond, just looked away sadly as a strained silence settled over the table.

Everyone at the school knew that Eleanor's Door was waiting for her, that it had never stopped waiting for her, and she'd be able to go back to her Nonsense world as soon as her thoughts softened enough to accept the chaos without breaking down. The world she'd traveled to had left her aging more slowly than the human norm, delaying that return, but had also granted her a certain elasticity of thought that would eventually make the transition easier for her. It was a balanced teeter-totter, currently falling more toward neither option.

"That's true enough," said Eleanor slowly. "Familial Doors are an oddity. I've only heard of a few apart from my own, and they tend to vanish after they've finished swallowing down the family members who suit them. Maybe mine will close itself forever after it takes me back. Kade's not suited, and there's no way of knowing whether any children of his would be."

Kade's cheeks flushed a pale shade of red at that, looking resolutely at the wall. "How do these family Doors handle adoption?" he asked.

"Every student who's come here has been my child, one way or another. The Weald and Wold hasn't called to any of them. I'm not sure the Doors know what to do with adoption."

"That's a little prejudiced of them," said Talia.

"No, that's a little inhuman of them," said Eleanor. "They aren't people, they don't think like people, and they don't understand people the way that actual people do."

"A Door that only takes girls took me," said Kade. "The familial Doors only understanding blood relations may be the most reasonable thing I've heard about them, and I've heard as much as there is to hear."

"We're getting away from the actual point, which is that I need people to help me," said Nancy. "Christopher, I think you're a great fit for helping the Halls of the Dead. You can play the ghosts away from us. You can be our shield."

"I hope I can." Christopher worked his fingers anxiously across the surface of his flute. "I mostly play for skeletons and roadkill. Actual ghosts may be a little bit of a stretch."

"I believe in you," said Nancy. She looked at Sumi, not quite meeting the other girl's eyes, like she couldn't really believe in Sumi at all—in her existence, which had to seem too much like a miracle to make any sense at all. "Sumi, you're—"

"I'm coming with you," said Sumi simply. "I think that's all that really matters, don't you? If I say I'm coming? I've been to more worlds than I think anyone else at this school, and sometimes waking up under the same sky two days in a row is the hardest thing I've ever done. Plus I'm pretty good at fighting stuff. If Chris gets to be your shield, I get to be your sword, and I'll cut and I'll cut and I'll cut until there's nothing left for chopping."

"I've asked you not to call me that," said Christopher with surprising primness. "Just because you're happy being called by a nickname, that doesn't mean I am. My name is my name, just the way it is, not truncated to make it easier for you."

Sumi huffed quietly, turning to look at Eleanor like she thought she'd find help from that quarter.

Eleanor only shook her head. "Names matter, dear. If someone wants to be called something, that's what you call them, whether or not it's what you would want to be called in their place."

"Fine. Chris*to*pher can be the shield, and I'll chop and chop," said Sumi.

"Thank you," said Christopher.

Sumi stuck out her tongue at him.

"Kade . . ." Nancy hesitated. "You didn't go to an Underworld, and you've never shown much of an affinity for the dead."

"No, but I can keep Sumi under control, and right now that feels like a skill you're dearly going to need on this little expedition," said Kade.

"Fair enough," agreed Nancy. She turned to look at Talia, who looked challengingly back.

"I'm not a shield and I'm not a sword and I can't control Sumi," she said. "I'm just coming with you, because the people who go on quests are the people who find their way home again, and I need to go home before it's too late for me. So I'm coming, whether you like it or not."

"What skills do you have?"

"I can weave a silk thread into anything if I try hard enough, and my pockets are full of silkworm cocoons. I can see in the dark, and I can talk to moths. I was trained to be a court poet, and record the history of the worlds so that it can be added to the reprises." Talia continued to look at her challengingly. "I'm coming with you."

"All right," said Nancy. "What's your name?"

"My English name is Talia, and that's what I prefer the people here call me," she said. "My birth name is Ming-Yue."

Nancy inclined her head, so deeply that it looked like the beginning of a bow. "All right," she said again. "I'm exhausted after the day I've had. Is there a place I can lie down for a while before we start trying to find the door back to the Halls of the Dead?"

"Of course, darling," said Eleanor. "Sumi doesn't have a roommate right now. You can have your own bed back."

"I even promise not to masturbate while you're in the room!" chirped Sumi, and there was nothing Nancy could do but laugh. She was back, all right. School was exactly as it had always been.

6 PERCHANCE TO DREAM

AFTER LUNCH WAS FINISHED and the dishes tidied away, Sumi seized Nancy's hand, chirped, "In case you don't remember the way," and pulled her out of the room, leaving the others behind. It was easier not to resist, and so Nancy let herself be pulled, out of the dining hall and toward the nearest flight of stairs, Sumi chattering a mile a minute about everything that had happened since she'd left the school.

Some of it didn't make any sense at all, body thefts and skeleton keys and resurrections—so many resurrections, it was like the people who went to this school thought death was something optional, something to be recovered from, and Nancy could admire their conviction, if not their flippant approach to something so important—and stores operated by talking birds from another reality. By the time they reached the room they had once shared, Nancy was exhausted just from *listening.*

Sumi opened the door and waved her inside, as grandly as if she were welcoming her to a palace. Nancy moved straight toward her old bed, which was neatly made if slightly dusty, and delicately folded forward, landing facedown on the waiting pillow.

"You *are* tired," said Sumi. "Do you want another blanket? Only you're on top of the one the bed comes with, and I don't know how squirmy you're feeling."

Nancy made a noncommittal noise.

"Okay," said Sumi. "I don't need to take your shoes off because you're not wearing shoes, but I'll get you that blanket."

Nancy didn't respond.

Sumi left the room and went down the hall to the closet, removing one of the spare blankets and bringing it back to the room. Nancy was already asleep, somehow even more motionless than she normally was. Sumi spread the blanket over her, not bothering to tuck it in, then stepped back to just look at her former roommate, watching her sleep.

A small frown on her face, she turned and walked out of the room, leaving Nancy to her rest.

Like many of the Nonsense children who genuinely wanted to go back through their doors, Sumi wore her bright colors and irreverent comments like they were a shield, but she was still the girl she'd been before Confection, would always be that girl on some level, no matter how hard she tried to bury her in a shallow grave at the back of her mind and forget what it had been like to brush her hair and confine her feet in sensible, somewhat uncomfortable shoes. She was haunted, as they all were. Her ghost was just quieter than most.

Maybe it was seeing Nancy again, but that ghost was awake, and asking all the questions she didn't want to hear. Questions like *You always say you're not afraid because you know you're going back to Confection to have your daughter when you're ready, but don't you remember how cold it was in the Halls of the Dead? How lonely you were? That's where the ghosts rise. Who's to say I won't rise up with them?* And *Can you really trust Talia on a quest? She's a poet, not a warrior. You could be leading her right into danger.*

She didn't like those questions any more than she liked the voice of her former self, who was normally content to haunt her memories and leave her to get on with the messy, delicious business of being alive. So she walked back to the dining hall, hoping to catch at least some of the others before they scattered.

What she found was Kade, still picking at his chicken, head hanging low in that way she knew meant he was giving altogether too much thought to something heavy. His thoughts weighed him down a lot, and she guessed that was a good thing, when he wanted to be anchored to the world where he was living, not drifting aimlessly and waiting for a Door that might never open.

She threw herself into the chair next to him, hard enough that she virtually assaulted it, and planted her elbows on the table. Kade looked up. Sumi grinned at him, wide and wild and white as anything. Her teeth were made of white peppermint, and had been since her resurrection; they couldn't decay, and didn't stain. Her smile would have been the envy of Hollywood, and all she had to do was die.

"How's it going, Kade?" she chirped. She eyed the mess on his plate. "Did your chicken make you angry? Only you seem to be stabbing more than swallowing, and that's not the greatest way to get full. Unless you're on a diet. More diets should be violence-based. Why do we call them diets when everybody has one? I'm on a diet of almost entirely sugar, but that doesn't mean I'm trying to lose weight. Justice for the word 'diet'! Free it from the chains of the weight loss industry!"

Kade listened to all this with a weary, accepting smile, letting her words wash over him, as he so often did. Out of everyone at the school, Kade was the happiest to sit and simply be babbled at, a willing receptacle for all the nonsense she wanted to spill. Even Eleanor never wanted to listen that long, and she adored Eleanor, the first adult child of Nonsense she'd ever met.

"You got a point in all that, Sumi, or do I just need to be a good listening ear? I can manage, if that's what you're wanting."

"I want to know why you're not eating, and why you look so sad," said Sumi.

"That's a complicated question."

"I'm a pretty straightforward girl, so no matter how complicated it is, I bet I'll be able to find a way through it. Try me."

Kade sighed, putting down his fork. "You don't know how to take no for an answer, do you?"

"I do," said Sumi, sounding faintly affronted. "People I want to have sex with tell me no all the time, and I always respect that. Some people don't want me to touch them, and I respect that too. But when my friends want to get stuck and sucked into the molasses swamps of being sad, I don't think it's bad or wrong or pushing the boundaries of consent to try and convince them to talk to me. Toddlers have to wear coats in the winter, children need to get enough vitamin C to skip scurvy, and teenagers sometimes need to talk about our feelings. It's the medicinal part of being a person. I know it sucks. Now answer the complicated question."

Kade sighed heavily. "You know I love you, right, Sumi?"

"Sure do," chirped Sumi. "If I weren't already getting married to Ponder just as soon as I'm ready to be a mother, you'd probably be trying to wife me up by now. We'd bake beautiful babies together, you and me."

For a moment, Kade's expression twisted, like he was trying to puzzle his way through what she'd just said. Then he let the moment go, and frowned, and asked, "Sumi, you *do* know where babies come from, don't you?"

"I know where they come from for people who are made

out of flesh and blood and sinew," she said. "I'm modeling chocolate-and-cereal treats on a scaffold of bone. Am I going to have Rini the normal way, or am I going to have to travel to the Baker and assemble her from scratch? That's the part I don't know, and I don't think anybody can. It's too strange a question to have ever been answered before. I'll find out eventually." She rolled one shoulder in half a shrug, and added, "Stop trying to dodge the question. Why do you look so sad?"

Kade scowled at her for a moment, then sighed again. "Nancy's back."

"I know. I just put her to bed."

"Nancy's back, and Nancy was the first of us to be absolutely bone-sure enough to find her door back to where she believed she belonged. She was the one who showed everyone else that it could be done. And look at us now. Jack and Jill, Cora, Antsy—even Stephanie, I guess, even though she never made it to the school. She was sure, she believed, she went home."

"Don't forget Nadya," said Sumi.

"Nadya didn't find her door. We abandoned her in the Halls of the Dead in exchange for your ghost so Rini could finish her quest to bring you back." He paused when he was finished speaking, looking briefly baffled by the words that had come out of his own mouth.

"Wait," said Sumi, sitting up a little straighter, eyes going wide with the kind of realization that only follows something you already know being restated in a way that makes it begin to make sense. "Wait-wait-wait. You left Nadya in the Halls of the Dead."

"Yes?"

"And the ghosts in those Halls are all angry and eating people up like bonbons," said Sumi with growing urgency. "Oh, we need the ghostie-girl to be as sure as snowflakes when she wakes up, because we need to get to Nadya while she still has skin."

Kade blinked, a flicker of alarm entering his own eyes. "I didn't even think about that," he said.

"But we said we'd let her sleep, so now you get to tell me why Nancy being back makes you sad."

Kade slumped. It was clear from the way his mouth twisted that he had momentarily believed he was going to get out of explaining his unhappiness, and was now even more unhappy because that wasn't happening. "I guess because if she was so sure and now she's back, how can any of us be sure of anything?"

Sumi smacked him in the shoulder.

"Ow!" Kade rubbed his shoulder, frowning at her. "What gives?"

"You were being stupid, and I have permission to smack you whack you when you're being stupid," said Sumi primly. "It's a strange sort of permission, but you gave it to me yourself, and I've held on to it. Nancy *was* sure she belonged in the Halls of the Dead. She still *is* sure. She's just even more sure that she doesn't want to die. People are big enough to hold more than one certainty at the same time. You're allowed to feel conflicted. You're allowed to think, *Oh maybe this time she'll stay*, and *Oh maybe people change their minds and someday I'll want to go back to Prism after all*. But even if she isn't here forever, it's better to be glad she's here now than it is to be sad because her being here makes you think some thoughts different than you thought them the first time."

"I guess you're right," said Kade reluctantly. "I'll try."

"Good," said Sumi. "Now stop stabbing your chicken and swallow it instead. We have a long way to go before you're going to see anything this nice again. I can't imagine they have a decent kitchen in a place that feeds people pomegranate juice and calls it Sunday dinner."

She leaned over, patting Kade gently on the head, then threw herself out of her chair and ran gleefully for the door, pigtails bouncing with every bounding step. Kade watched her go and smiled, turning back to his dinner.

She was right about one thing: they probably weren't going to get any decent meals in the Halls of the Dead.

CHRISTOPHER CIRCLED THE conservatory, flute in hand, watching the well-lit glass panes for signs of movement. They were constant, to some degree: moths landed on the windows, fanned their wings, and then took off again, flitting away on unknowable moth errands.

He paused when he reached the door, squinting into the brightness before he opened it and slipped through the sheet of slashed, hanging plastic on the other side. It was intended to keep the moths from escaping before they were ready, but it always made him feel like he was walking through a human car wash.

He emerged out the other side, into the conservatory proper. As he had hoped, Talia was there at her workbench, meticulously unwinding lengths of thread from a silkworm cocoon and wrapping them around her fingers like reminders set against the future. She looked so focused and intent that for a moment, he considered turning around and going back the way he'd come; he hated to be interrupted when he was in the zone. Presumably this was something similar. She was exercising the gift her Door had given her, something no one else in this world could possibly understand.

He took a step forward instead, then stopped, waiting patiently for her to acknowledge him. When she didn't, he took another step, still trying to make his presence known without startling her.

Talia snipped a bit of thread. "I know you're there, Flores. You can just tell me what you want. And if what you want is to convince me that I should stay behind while the rest of you go save the world—any world—then I will tell you where you can stuff it."

"You're a lot less shy and wispy than you always came across in therapy," said Christopher.

Talia shrugged. "Seraphina's in half my sessions. I didn't want her paying attention to me. So I played up the shy and wispy parts of my journey, I guess. Maybe you should have paid more attention to what I was saying, and less to how it was being said."

"Maybe," said Christopher. "Look, I'm not your boyfriend, brother, or dad. It's not my job to convince you that a field trip to a place called the Halls of the Dead is a bad idea. If Cora were still here, she'd probably be trying, but she always cared an awful lot more than I did."

"You don't care if I die?"

"Talia, I don't care if *anyone* dies, as long as it gets me one step closer to my Skeleton Girl."

Talia gave him a strange look. Like everyone else who had discussed Mariposa with Christopher, she knew what his reunion with the girl he loved was going to mean—maybe not death in the classical sense, since he would still be thinking and talking and moving around, but close enough. He wouldn't be like Nancy, returning to the school if his conviction wavered. He would be a citizen of Mariposa forever, with no way back across the border.

If that was what he wanted, it was difficult to begrudge him his happy ending. But oh, that happy ending looked like a horror movie to anyone standing on the other side of the wall.

"Good," she said curtly.

Christopher sighed, looking around the conservatory. This wasn't going as well as he'd been hoping it would; he'd somehow expected her to drop her defenses and open up immediately, welcoming him as the friend he was trying to be. He should have paused to realize how large the gulf between the girl he'd thought he knew and the real person would have to be for her to insert herself into their quest the way she already had. He should have done this better.

Everywhere he looked, there were dead moths. They weren't so thick on the ground as to make him think that Talia was doing something wrong; far more were in the air. But they were delicate, short-lived creatures, and some of them would always fall and die before they could be released. Once his eyes adjusted to the shape of them, scattered like so many dead leaves, they became impossible to ignore.

He ran his fingers along the surface of his flute, feeling the indentations arrayed in place of holes. "Do you want some help cleaning up in here?" he asked.

"Knock yourself out," said Talia.

Christopher nodded, raised his flute, and began to play.

On the first note, the dead moths twitched.

On the second, the first few opened their wings.

On the third, they began taking to the air.

By the time he finished the first silent phrase of his song, he was surrounded by a glowing cloud of moths, their tattered wings beating double-fast to keep them aloft as they circled his head. A few, too damaged to fly, walked or crawled across the ground toward him, swarming over his feet and climbing his legs to get closer to the music.

Perhaps it was the motion that caught her attention. Talia turned to look at him, and froze, staring open-mouthed at the expanding cloud of dead insects that surrounded him. As for Christopher, he remained where he was and kept on playing until every one of the moths was either clinging to his clothing or circling his head, then turned, still playing, to walk toward the door.

"Wait!" exclaimed Talia, throwing her hand out in front of her. Christopher glanced back at her, still playing. "I can . . . I can open the back door, so you won't knock any of them off," she said, and dug into her pocket, producing a key. "Follow me."

She ran across the conservatory to a small locked door half-hidden behind some trees, brushing a few living moths away from the frame. Christopher nodded and followed after her, more slowly to allow the dead moths to keep up with him.

Talia opened the door and he stepped outside, playing a long, trilling note that no ears of flesh could hear, but that the moths somehow responded to. The ones who could fly spiraled upward and outward, scattering into the evening air, while the ones who couldn't dropped from his clothing to the ground, spreading their wings wide before finally lying still.

A few living moths fluttered out the open door and were lost to the sky, unnoticed by either Talia or Christopher. She did close the door, still staring at him.

Satisfied that the moths were gone, Christopher lowered his flute and turned to fully face her.

"Anyway," he said. "Welcome aboard."

Hesitantly, Talia smiled.

PART II

A CLOSED CASKET

7 LOCKS AND UNLOCKS

EVERY TIME NANCY HAD managed to find a Door to the Halls of the Dead, it had been located belowground. The first had been in the basement of the house she'd shared with her parents; the second had been in her basement bedroom at the school. Two wasn't a large group to generalize from, but it was a better sample size than one.

The group that intended to travel with her packed themselves into the rarely used root cellar below the kitchen, where the air smelled of good, clean earth and the corners were thick with cobwebs, some of them years old. Nancy approached the wall, where there was no door, not even a crack or outline of same, and lifted her hand, letting her fingertips rest gently against the hard-packed dirt.

"I don't know what I'm supposed to do now," she admitted.

"Just *want*," Sumi advised. "Think back to when you were a kid and you wanted something with all your heart and all your thoughts at the same time, when the wanting was so big it ate the whole world. You need that wanting."

"I don't know if I *can* want that way anymore," said Nancy. "I think once you start growing up, other things begin getting in the way of the wanting, the same way the older you are, the more things there are between you and being absolutely all-the-way sure."

"But you *are* sure, aren't you?" asked Kade.

Nancy closed her eyes, tucking her chin toward her chest. "I'm *so* sure," she said. "The Halls of the Dead are my home, and I want to go home more than anything. I want to find out why the ghosts are so angry that they're hurting the living statues, that they're tearing through all the rules and traditions we have to keep everyone safe. There's room for us all in the Halls, but the dead decided they should have more room than the living, and they started taking it. That's not right. It's not the way things are supposed to be. I'm sure I want to find a way to set things right again."

As she spoke, thin lines of light began to form on the wall, gradually coming together to form the glowing outline of a door. It was smooth and elegantly drawn, like an architectural sketch. Nancy finished talking and leaned forward until her forehead was resting against the dirt, eyes still closed. She sighed, sounding weary beyond all measure.

And as her forehead made contact with the wall, the door that had appeared there creaked ever so slightly open. No more than a few inches, barely wide enough to let someone slip a hand inside, but for a door stitching together two worlds, that was more than enough.

The wind that whispered through the cracked door was cold and bright, and smelled of pomegranates. Nancy's eyes snapped open, and she straightened, staring at the outlined door.

"Did you just emo your way into finding the Door home?" asked Sumi. "Because that's a pretty good trick, if that's what you did."

Nancy ignored her, turning wide eyes on the top of the door, gaze running along the line of it to the point where a doorknob would have been, if there were going to be one at all. Not seeing anything of the sort, she pressed her palm flat against the dirt wall, well within the outline, and pushed inward, hard.

The door swung open, and the pomegranate grove was revealed, dark-leafed trees reaching for the star-speckled sky like hungry hands. The grass, green as ever, was dotted with fallen pomegranates. Nancy took a step forward, until she was half over the threshold and half not, straddling the two worlds. She looked back at her companions.

"Are you coming?" she asked.

They moved forward, the four of them sticking close together. Even Sumi looked anxious, taking hold of the tail of Kade's shirt and holding it fast as she allowed him to lead her onward to the threshold.

"You don't have to," said Nancy. "I can figure this out by myself if I have to. I'll be okay."

"You were not-okay enough to come looking for help," said Kade. "But you're still sure enough to open a door home. I think we need to come with you. I think we'd be rotten friends if we let you go and try to do this by yourself."

Nancy smiled, a little wryly. "Like I was a rotten friend when I left you and didn't even say goodbye? Sometimes we're all rotten friends. Sometimes the right thing to do is to let people deal with their own mistakes."

"Not this time," said Kade, and when Nancy walked through the door into the moonlit grove on the other side, he was right behind her, dragging Sumi in his wake. Christopher and Talia came close behind them.

Only Talia seemed to hear the door in the root-cellar wall slamming closed again. She turned in time to see it disappear, the rectangle cut out of the air simply vanishing like it had never existed to begin with. She swallowed hard, and turned back to the others.

Too late to turn back now.

NANCY SPREAD HER ARMS, still moving with that stop-motion eeriness, and let her head drop back, eyes closing again as she breathed in the sweet, cold evening air. Around her, the others performed their own examinations of the space. Sumi moved to the nearest tree, giving it a solid shake, and squealed with delight when pomegranates showered down to thump into the grass, some of them splitting open at the point of impact and scattering garnet seeds in all directions. The shaking knocked several moths loose at the same time, and they took to the air, gray upper wings lifting to show bright orange lower wings. Talia laughed and spread her arms, and the moths fluttered down to land on them, antennae waving.

Christopher raised his flute and played a swift, silent arpeggio before he nodded, apparently satisfied. "I can feel my audience listening," he said. "There are plenty of dead things here."

"The ghosts and the statues share the pomegranate grove, when we have to," said Nancy. "They don't attack us here, and we don't stand so still that we fool them into thinking we don't matter. We just coexist."

"If they're attacking you in the halls, can we be sure they'll follow the rules here?" asked Kade.

"The trees will enforce them," said Nancy almost dreamily.

Sumi paused in the act of picking up a pomegranate from the ground, shooting a wary glance at the nearest tree. Its branches were gnarled and dark, like wrought iron sculptures decked in leaves and jeweled fruit. "Enforce them how?" she asked.

"They have their ways, and I'm not a garden statue. I never asked," said Nancy. "Still, you're right that we shouldn't linger here. The other statues will be inside. We should go to them."

"Yes," said Kade without conviction. If Nancy had survived by fleeing to another world, he wasn't sure any of her companions would still be in their places. Still, they were here to help her, and that meant letting her lead the way.

Nancy turned, and there, where the undefined edge of the grove had been a moment before, was a tall white stone wall, and a beautiful silver gateway leading to the manicured grounds of the hall beyond. The hall was Grecian in design, but not as old-fashioned as he would have expected; there was something distinctly modern about its design, like it was made from all the dreams of the Grecian underworld spread thin across the centuries. Nancy started toward the gate and the rest of them followed, even Talia's moths, which had been joined by another dozen or so of their fellows.

Sumi skipped ahead, a pomegranate in either hand, and paced alongside Nancy. "Can I eat these?" she demanded. "Or will I owe your spooky Lord a month for every seed?"

"You're not the Lady, and neither am I," said Nancy. "She was the only one he ever bartered for that way, and people forget how hard it is to break into a pomegranate that's anything other than perfectly, skin-splittingly ripe. She didn't eat those seeds by accident, or without understanding what she was doing. Eat whatever you like. It isn't going to hold you here."

"Great," said Sumi, and took a large bite out of the split

fruit, seeds and pulp and skin. She crunched for a moment, then wrinkled her nose and began spitting bits of leathery pomegranate skin onto the grass, still crunching seeds between her teeth.

Nancy smiled indulgently at her. "It's so nice to see you alive again," she commented.

Talia, at the rear of the group, looked confused, turning to Christopher. "What?" she asked.

"Sumi was dead for a while," he said.

"I thought that was metaphorical, or one of those things where someone has a heart attack and has to be shock-paddled back to life."

"Nope. She was murdered by someone we thought was a friend of ours, and she died and stayed dead for a good while before we needed her to be alive again. I think that was really the first quest: getting Sumi back from the afterlife." The girl in question was skipping circles around Nancy, still taking bites out of her pomegranate and spitting skin on the ground like this was perfectly normal.

"That's . . . Wow." Talia shook her head. "Sumi never stops talking. Like, I think she even talks in her sleep. How did I not know this?"

"Sumi tries to shy away from the serious stuff when she's just talking to hear herself talk. It's too hard to be nonsensical and tragic at the same time, and she's not taking any risks with her essential nature. But yeah, she was dead, and she would have stayed dead if Nancy hadn't helped us find her spirit."

"Oh," said Talia, eyes wide as she looked at Nancy again. "Have any of the rest of you been dead?"

"Us? Nah. Kade's a goblin prince, and I'm engaged to a

skeleton, but neither of us have been dead. And Nancy never needed to die. She just needed to know that death loved her, and she knows that better than anyone else I know."

They were nearing the great Grecian hall. As they stepped into the manicured gardens, low hedges and beautiful topiary stretching out all around them, the first of the statues appeared.

They were dressed like Nancy, in flowing white chitons and chitoniskos, but unlike Nancy, none of the garden statues in sight had any colored accents; compared to them, her little dashes of red were impossibly bright, shockingly daring. Most of them were white-haired, although a few had the same striped patterning as she did, the fingers of the Lord of the Dead permanently branded in their tresses. One man had streaks of carroty orange surrounded by white, while a girl had streaks of chestnut brown.

There was something inherently vital about the statues, even though they didn't move, didn't blink or visibly breathe; still, passing among them, it was obvious that they were alive. Sumi stared at them with unabashed fascination, looking them up and down without blinking. "What happens if it rains?" she asked. "Or if there's a bad wind? Or if there's bees?"

"It doesn't rain here," said Nancy patiently. "There are windstorms, but only three times a year, and we always have notice when they're coming, so we can move all the garden statues inside. And the only bees here are corpse bees, which are harmless to the living. It's still hard to hold still when one lands on your eyeball."

Kade shuddered. "In a world of horrors, that's the most upsetting thing you've ever said," he accused. "Maybe don't."

"Fair enough," said Nancy. She stopped in front of one of the statues, a burly man whose hair was chalky white but whose beard was ruddy red, encompassing his chin and jawline. "Lief, I'm sorry, but I need someone to tell me what's been happening for the last two weeks."

Christopher jerked slightly, startled by her request, then paused, doing the math in his head. If a month on Earth was equivalent to a year in the Halls of the Dead, then a day on Earth would be roughly equal to twelve days in the Halls. Nancy had been with them for a day, but she'd been gone from her friends and the danger posed by the riled-up ghosts for nearly two weeks.

Bit by bit, so slowly that it looked more like a special effect than anything real, the man she'd called Lief began to move. He subtly angled himself toward Nancy, then melted gradually into a crouching position, expression never changing. Once he was closer to her level, he stopped, weight now balanced on his toes and the fingers of one pale hand.

"Your friend . . . has fruit," he said, each word ponderous as a boulder rolling down a hill. "Three . . . seeds."

"Sumi, give him three seeds," said Nancy. She turned so that she was facing the others, and said, "It can be hard to speak after a long posing session, unless you have something to moisten your throat. The seeds will make it easier for him."

Christopher nodded. Kade looked uncomfortable.

Carefully, Sumi plucked three seeds from her ravaged pomegranate and set them on the plinth next to Lief's hand. He reached down with his other hand, picking them up and bringing them to his mouth. Every motion took an age. Nancy held perfectly still, watching him, and somehow his slow, stuttering movement drove home even more how unnatural her own stillness was. When she froze, she might as well have been carved from marble. None of the little motions that defined the living were present in her face.

Lief chewed, once, crushing the seeds between his teeth, then swallowed and returned his attention to Nancy. "I had heard one of the Lady's attendant statues was removed from the world," he said. "Was that you?"

"Unless she was able to see another to safety," said Nancy. "What happened? What continues to happen?"

"The unquiet dead have found themselves a champion," said Lief. "A newly arrived spirit so filled with rage at the reality of death that they have been antagonizing the other ghosts, rallying them to break from their chambers and sweep through the halls. Where they find signs of life they rip apart and devour of it. Some of them have consumed enough of the living to appear as shades, shaped now like the people they were in life. Some have taken enough to remember their names."

"That isn't right," said Nancy, sounding stricken. "How many of the statues have they killed?"

"Thus far, the dead remain inside the halls. The garden statuary is safe." He sounded lightly smug as he said that.

Nancy frowned a little, casting her eyes downward. "There's no need to gloat at the misfortune of your peers," she said, chiding lightly.

"The interior statues have held themselves superior to us for long enough that if we want to take pleasure in being spared such a vast and terrible danger, we should be allowed our small satisfaction," he said. "But you're right. The indoor statues did nothing to deserve or cause this, and they deserve our sympathy in these hours."

"Thank you."

Lief inclined his head. "I apologize for my insensitivity. But since your departure, the attacks have continued. When last we were brought news, fully half the interior statues were gone, and the Lady was offering to escort any who wished to avoid a similar fate to the groves, where they might find their own doorways home. I think she may have forgotten the exchange of time between our world and yours."

Something about the way he said that made Sumi stop picking at her pomegranates and frown at him. He looked impassively back.

"You're not from Earth, are you?" she asked. "You're like Ponder. You're a person shaped like a people who didn't start out on the world we come from. Where are you from?"

"I was born in a place called the Goblin Market, where everything has a price and all life is lived according to the principles of fair value," said Lief. "I grew tired of bartering for my existence before I was ten years old, and when I saw a door that seemed likely to take me away from there, I took it. I have never once looked back. This is where I was meant to be from the beginning. I just started out in the wrong place."

Sumi, who had heard of the Goblin Market before, nodded. "We had a teacher who'd traveled there, once. She died, and she didn't get better. It was very sad."

"Death often is," Lief said. He returned his attention to Nancy. "The Lord and Lady walk the Halls, agitated and angry. They have barred the doors against new arrivals, forbidding any intrusion to their holdings. They must have left a loophole for your return."

"I was sent to fetch help," said Nancy.

"Have you?"

"I think so." She gestured to the people behind her, and that motion was more fluid than it would have been when she first returned to the school, although it was still stop-motion staccato; she was beginning to recover the habit of movement. "Sumi was a resident here, before her own resurrection; the quiet dead may remember her, and be willing to come to her aid. Christopher can pipe the dead to dance at his command; there's every chance he can stop the attacks if he has time to raise his flute. Kade is a goblin prince from a far-off Fairyland, and he has the way of command about him. And Talia is a poet. Poets have always possessed special powers in the lands of the dead. We just need to ask the Lady what she demands of us."

"The unquiet dead swept through the atrium some hours ago," said Lief. "We could hear the screams from here. It seems unlikely that they would return so soon, with all the Halls open for their feasting."

"Thank you," said Nancy. She turned to the others as Lief began the slow, laborious process of straightening, returning to the standing position he had occupied when she first addressed him. "If the Lady has not yet evacuated the Halls, it's close enough to safe for us to enter."

"Because *that's* a reasonable way to measure safety," muttered Talia. "Whether the woman who encourages people to turn themselves into literal statues has decided she needs to evacuate her house."

"Works for me," chirped Sumi.

Nancy turned toward the hall, took a deep breath, and started walking forward.

The rest of them followed, a train of moths fluttering along behind them.

8 LADY OF THE DEAD

THEY STEPPED THROUGH THE unlocked front door of the hall, and immediately Christopher understood why this place was called the Halls of the Dead when everything else they'd seen up to this point had been so blazingly, brutally alive. There was a mausoleum stillness in the air, like nothing had disturbed it in a hundred years, and the marble walls were softened by velvet draperies that swallowed the sounds of their footsteps so completely that they effectively became silence. The ceiling was so high that it felt like walking into a vault, and like the space should have been as full of echoes as it was of light. Their absence was jarring enough to make itself noticeable.

Plinths studded the round room around them, one every four or five feet, all of them polished white marble . . . and all of them empty. Christopher peered closer, then recoiled as he spotted a dot of reddish brown on one of the plinths. As soon as he saw that first one, more appeared, blossoming out of the whiteness like terrible flowers.

Dried blood. All of the plinths had been lightly misted with blood at some point, and whoever had cleaned them hadn't been able to get it all.

Still, the group walked forward, Talia allowing the door to slam shut behind her. Even that sound, large as it was, was no match for the silence: it was swallowed down as quickly as everything else, vanishing into the maw of the stillness.

Talia walked a little faster, drawing level to Christopher. One of the moths was perched at her temple, fanning its wings like a strange, living hair clip.

"I don't think I like it here," she said. "I don't think we're supposed to *be* here."

"It always feels like that when you go to a world that didn't call you," he said. "It's fine. Nancy wouldn't have brought us here if it weren't safe."

"And it is safe, most of the time," said a voice from behind them.

The four travelers who had accompanied Nancy whipped around, all of them moving fast and fluid and terrified. Nancy turned more slowly, with engrained elegance, and was already smiling as she began the long process of bowing to the speaker.

The silence had swallowed more than just their arrival: it had also taken the approach of the woman now standing in the middle of the room, smiling indulgently at them, like they were adorable children who had wandered somewhere they weren't supposed to be.

She was short, taller only than Sumi, and lushly curved, with skin a few shades darker than Christopher's and long, dark hair that fell in curls down her back. Her eyes were the same red as the pomegranate seeds, an impossibly deep color that had no business appearing in human eyes.

But Christopher looked at her and knew that she wasn't human, just like the Skeleton Girl wasn't human; she was the closest thing he'd seen to his beloved since leaving Mariposa. He didn't know how that could be true, when this woman had skin and fat and muscle and organs, but he knew that it *was* true, and that truth would have told him at once who she was, even if he hadn't met her once before.

"My Lady," he said, and bowed. Kade did the same, and after a puzzled beat, Sumi and Talia followed suit.

When they straightened, the Lady of the Dead was still smiling, although the expression had become tempered by a sliver of concern. "Nancy, you're back," she said. "Are these the people you brought to help you quiet the dead?"

"They are," said Nancy. "I used to go to school with them, and they volunteered their aid. No one is here against their will, and they understand the depth of the danger they're subjecting themselves to by coming."

"But they're that willing to take the risk if it means they can help a friend? You inspired loyalty while you walked among the living, my Nancy," said the Lady of the Dead.

Sumi frowned, looking oddly shy. "I . . . know you," she said. "Why do I know you?"

"Because, little ghost, this is where you came when your first body died. I met you in the pomegranate grove, and plucked you from the air, and brought you here, brought you home, so you could rest and recover yourself before you went onward to another life. But it seems you've chosen to continue the life you had before. An unusual selection, if not unheard-of."

"Oh," said Sumi.

"All of you need to come with me," said the Lady. "You're in great danger if you linger in the open. Our private chambers have been sealed against the disembodied, and that should hold for a time—long enough for a solution to be found, we hope."

"Have all the others gone back to their original worlds?" asked Nancy.

The Lady of the Dead frowned, lips drawing delicately downward. "No, my love. You were the only one who made it to their door."

Nancy blinked, but gave no other outward sign of her distress.

"Come," said the Lady, and began to walk. The group followed her, through the silent halls, toward the promise of safety.

IT WASN'T A LONG JOURNEY, but the quiet, combined with the invisible threat from all around, made it feel longer than the walk from the pomegranate grove to the gardens. The Lady of the Dead walked with quiet confidence, never pausing, never looking back. Nancy walked with the same economy of motion she had been demonstrating since her arrival at the school, like she was only allowed so much movement during any given day and didn't want to run out in the middle of a step, one foot lifted in preparation of a descent that would never come.

The rest of them simply walked, clustering closely together, even Sumi holding back the urge to skip or circle or roam ahead. Instead, she stayed at Kade's side, slightly behind him, eyes flicking constantly from place to place as she tried to watch the entire hallway at the same time.

As they reached a junction in the hall, another corridor crossing over theirs, she abruptly stiffened, grabbing Kade's arm. "Kade," she said, in a tightly controlled voice, "you know how sometimes I say things just for the sake of saying them, and they don't mean anything at all, really, except that I'm here and I have a voice and I can say whatever I like?"

"Yes?" he replied.

"This isn't one of those times. *Run*."

She broke away from him then, running forward until she was trotting alongside the Lady of the Dead. "I hope we're close to where we're going, because we need to get there *now*," she said.

The Lady of the Dead frowned at her, and began to turn, clearly intending to ask Kade what she was on about. The motion brought her, briefly, into position to look down the crossing corridor, and her own eyes widened. She reached back, grabbing Nancy by the hand. "Run," she said, with less panic and more authority than Sumi, and began running down the hallway, hauling Nancy along with her.

The rest of the travelers followed, not sure what they were running for, only sure that anything capable of putting that look on the Lady's face was something they didn't want to play around with. Sumi looked back as she ran, the color draining from her face with every backward glance.

Christopher looked back, trying to see if he could figure out what they were running from, and saw nothing but a slight haziness in the air, like the distortion that sometimes appeared above asphalt on a hot summer's day. But the hall wasn't hot. It wasn't cold, either. It was perfectly temperate, like standing inside a well-designed and climate-controlled shopping mall. Too much heat or cold would have been hard on the statues, making it impossible for them to hold their places.

So he kept running, and the others ran with him. Some of Talia's moths were dislodged by her flight along the hall, fluttering behind the group as they worked to catch up. As Christopher glanced back again, he saw the rearmost moths beginning to dissolve.

It wasn't an instantaneous process. The moths were flying, flapping their wings in their effort to catch back up to Talia, and then they were gone, the dissolution moving from the backs of their bodies up to the feathers of their antennae. In less than a second, each moth caught this way had been reduced to nothing but a thin cloud of ashy-looking dust that floated in the air for a moment before drifting, lifeless, to the marble floor.

It was easier to run when he knew that was behind them, and the others seemed to feel similarly, because they surged forward, a united group, approaching a pair of ornately graven double doors patterned in pomegranate boughs and long, elegant stalks of grain, with roe deer hidden in the background, almost lost among the greenery.

The Lady of the Dead surged forward, pressing her hands against the double doors, which swung open easily, offering no resistance. "In!" she shouted, and it was an obscenity, to hear her raise her voice so; nothing in this world should have been able to make the Lady yell. "Get inside!"

The others didn't need to be told twice. They rushed through the open doors, even Nancy, who moved almost as quickly as Kade did, getting the others inside. Once they were all through, the Lady of the Dead stepped over the threshold into the room and stopped, panting. She didn't close the doors, only turned to glare defiantly out into the hall.

"Nothing in these Halls can cross my threshold without permission, and I do not grant it," she said.

There was a rushing sound, like some terrible wind was blowing through the halls, and then there was silence.

"I know you're there. If you're finally coming so close to my private chambers, you must be ready to issue your demands. So speak to me, unquiet spirits. Speak to your Lady, and tell me why you wreak such havoc in my Halls. I would prefer that it be ended."

The rushing of the wind returned, louder now, pressing right up against the threshold while the Lady stood there, expression patient and neutral.

Sumi inched forward, standing at the Lady's side. The Lady glanced at her, lifting an eyebrow. "I can see them," said Sumi. "Not very clearly-clearly, but enough to know they're there. I saw them before. That was how I knew to run."

"Sumi, you can see the dead people?" asked Kade.

"I was one of the dead people who haunt this place," said Sumi. "I guess it makes sense that I can still see them."

"None of the rest of us can," said Talia, after a quick glance around at the others. Nancy was panting, one hand pressed to her chest and an expression of dismay on her face as she failed to make the involuntarily hard breathing stop. Kade and Christopher were standing close together, both looking blankly at the door, eyes slightly unfocused in the way of people who weren't looking *at* anything, only staring in the direction of least resistance.

"I see nothing, my Lady," said Nancy, words broken up by her attempts to catch her breath.

As if she had invoked them, glimmering points of light began to appear in the hall in front of the open doors to the Lady's chambers. They sparkled silver, first hanging motionless and then beginning to dart from place to place, swirling around one another, filling the air with their shine.

Christopher's eyes widened, and he raised his flute. "I'm going to try something," he said, before he lifted it to his lips and began to play.

"Lovely music, dear," said the Lady of the Dead into the silence. "Perhaps something a trifle faster would be a good idea?"

Christopher nodded, unaccustomed to people commenting on his playing, and his fingers picked up speed, gliding across the bone with preternatural smoothness, never slowing or stilling.

The motes of light swirled faster, more and more of them appearing, until they began to coalesce directly in front of the doors. Bit by bit, they formed the figure of a translucent teenage girl, sketched in starlight and stripped of substance. She was almost the same height as Kade, with long pale hair gathered over one shoulder by a darker ribbon, arranged into a perfect cascade of soup-can curls. Her dress was long and flowing, an elegant Victorian confection that fell to her feet in a waterfall of ruffles and lace. She had no color beyond the silver that comprised it, and even in monochrome, densities of color were apparent: her hair was light, her ribbon dark, her dress lighter than her hair, and probably white.

A dark choker circled her throat, and if that hadn't been enough proof of her identity, the stains on her spectral fingers would have been. It looked almost like she had dipped her hands in paint before rendering them in silver, covering her natural skin tone in something deeper, something darker.

She was smiling, meeting the eyes of the Lady of the Dead with a calm, unflinching gaze, like she had every right, like they were equals. "Hello," she said, and her voice was hollow as a jack-o'-lantern, scooped clean of every scrap of its original vitality. Still, she was audible, and the air around her was full of dancing silver, and maybe vitality was overrated.

The Lady of the Dead scowled. "Go back to your rooms. You shame the dead with your behavior. You shame this house."

"How can I shame anything when I didn't do anything wrong?" asked the girl. "I was a child, and I died, and it wasn't fair, and if I want to fill my throat with life until my spirit remembers how to live, I should be allowed to do exactly that."

"My statues are not for you to slaughter."

"They die so easy, though," said the girl, and giggled

girlishly, hiding her mouth behind her hand. "If they were worth preserving, they wouldn't die so easily. They wouldn't taste so amazing. Is this what it's always like? Swallowing life? Why doesn't everyone do it?"

"Because if the dead consume the living, the living run out," said the Lady. "That isn't how things are meant to work, not here, and not anywhere else."

"Oh don't be *dull,*" said the shade. "There are so many worlds, and so many ways for things to go properly, you can't honestly tell me that there are no worlds where the dead are allowed to feast on the living to their hearts' desire. Let us in. Open your invisible door and let us in. I promise we'll be good."

"Hello, Jill," said Kade.

9 CLASS REUNION

SILENCE FOLLOWED KADE'S WELCOME, lingering for several terrible seconds before the ghost of Jillian Wolcott laughed with exaggerated, overblown delight, clapping her insubstantial hands.

"Teacher's pet!" she said. "I was wondering if I'd ever see you again!"

"Hello, Jill," said Sumi, stepping forward as she snapped out of her shock. "Guess the shroud's on the other foot now, huh?"

Jill stopped laughing. "I *killed* you," she said angrily. "I took your hands and your nonsense story, and I left you for dead. I saw you *die*. I saw your skeleton wrapped in rainbows, walking around like it didn't matter at all. You can't be here."

"Don't you remember seeing me again in the Moors, after you stole your sister's body like it was a coat you thought was really nice and wanted her to share? Because I remember seeing you. I put a baling hook in the throat of that man you called 'father,' and I didn't let him save you from the fall. I helped your sister take her body back, and I spoiled all your plans."

"Not all of them," said Jill with a shark's smile. "I have new plans now, and you can't spoil a single one. Come out of that room and I'll swallow you whole. We won't leave anything this time to resurrect."

"No thank you," said Sumi, shaking her head so hard that her pigtails whipped across her face like lashes.

"Coward," said Jill. She shifted her smile over to Nancy. "You were such good cover for what I was already intending to do. Before you came, I'd been planning to pin everything on Jack, to make her think she was sleepwalking and succumbing to the scalpel in the same breath. But you were better. Not connected to us, not *part* of us, not anyone's friend. No one was going to miss you. How did you get to win while I had to lose?"

"You're killing all my friends," said Nancy. "Is that really what winning looks like?"

"On the Moors, yes," said Jill. "What kind of life did they have anyway, spending all their time pretending to be objects of art? That's not a life. That's a *display*."

"No one gets to decide for you what living looks like," snapped Nancy. "Life is supposed to be made up of the choices you make for yourself. Some of us choose perpetual motion. Some of us choose stillness. Neither one is better than the other."

"Bah," said Jill. "I am *going* to have a life again. I am *going* to put myself back together, one molecule at a time, and then I am *going* home to show my sister how badly she messed up." She returned her attention to the Lady of the Dead. "You want to save your statues? You want your pretty toys? Find something else to feed me and my army. Because we are *legion*, and we are not going back into the dark."

She shot a withering look at the still-playing Christopher. "Stop," she commanded.

Startled, he did exactly that. The flecks of silver vanished, the free-floating ones first, and then Jill herself. She faded the same way she had appeared, a little bit at a time, until there was nothing remaining to show that she had ever been there.

Christopher lowered his flute, staring at the empty hall. Everyone else was doing the same, looking at the space where Jill had been like she might lunge for them at any moment. Only Sumi's eyes were fully focused; she could see the absence of the dead as easily as she had seen their presence.

"My Lady?" asked Nancy in a meek voice.

"Yes, Nancy?"

"Is there really nothing you can do?"

The Lady of the Dead reluctantly shook her head. "I wish there were, but my husband and I don't command the dead, only give them a waystation on their way to whatever comes next. We're not the only waystation of its kind, just the one where you are."

Nancy bit her lip. That small gesture was so thoughtlessly human that it made Kade ache to see it. It was like she was remembering that she was a living creature against this backdrop of tragedy, like running to save the people she cared about was reminding her that she *could* run.

"Where is he?" she asked.

"Who, my dear?" replied the Lady.

"Your husband," said Nancy. "Where is my Lord?"

THE DEAD WERE FAST, but the Lady knew all the spaces that were sealed against them, and both she and Sumi could see them coming, while Christopher could stop them as long as he was properly prepared to play. They moved through the halls as a tight cluster, Sumi and the Lady on constant watch for trouble, Nancy and Talia pressed into the middle, like they needed protecting.

Talia, who had finally noticed how many of her moths were missing as they prepared to leave the Lady's quarters, didn't comment on where she'd been positioned. She hadn't commented on much of anything since that moment. It was like she had suddenly realized why the school had a rule against quests, why they were considered verboten: she had been given exactly what she asked for, and, in receiving it, had discovered that there was a reason no one wanted what she had.

They moved quickly, the oasis of the Lady's quarters left far behind them as they made for the last place where the Lady had seen her Lord. The two of them had been spending most of their time apart since the unquiet dead broke loose, the Lady seeing to her statues and protecting what she could—although as they passed still-standing statues in the halls, Kade reflected grimly that "what she could" didn't seem to include inviting the statues into her private chambers where the dead would be unable to reach them—while the Lord tried to determine what had changed.

Well, they knew what had changed now, at least in part. Jill Wolcott had died twice, both times at her sister's hand, and if there was anyone primed to become a restless ghost, it was her. Maybe more importantly, between her first death and her second, she had used the lightning inherent to the Moors to knock her spirit loose from her flesh, transferring it first into her sister's body, and then back into her own. That had to change something in even a dead person's structure. There was just no way it wouldn't.

And like the rest of them, Jill Wolcott was a child of the

Doors. Like Sumi, she'd been pulled to the Halls after her final death, and joined the cloud of ghosts waiting to be released and reborn. But Jill had so much anger in her, it was no real surprise that she'd grown tired of waiting and decided that it was time to act.

All this was information the Lord of the Dead didn't have, and needed to have. And it would be reassuring to have him with them. To hear Nancy speak of him, he was barely shy of a god, a man with total dominion over his own realm, even if that dominion was partially shared with his wife.

It was the Lord of the Dead, not the Lady, who had turned Nancy's hair white with a touch. And it was the Lord of the Dead who had bargained with them for the release of Sumi's spirit. Kade hated to act as if the solution to a dangerous situation was to get a man, but in this specific case, that felt like the right thing to do. So they hurried through the halls, five teens and one woman a sliver shy of being a goddess, and they waited for an attack that didn't come.

Sumi paused a few times, apparently secure in her ability to see the dead coming, and peered up at the statues that lined the halls, studying their motionless faces.

"Why?" she asked, looking toward the Lady.

"Why what?" asked the Lady.

"Why, when you saw that the ghosts would kill and eat anyone they could catch, did you not bar the doors against travelers, or set up safe rooms where they could catch their breath before you sent them home? Why turn them into architecture?"

"You're a Nonsense creature. You couldn't possibly understand." The Lady opened a door, waving them all anxiously through.

"Try me," suggested Sumi.

"The doors called them here because this was their natural home. We just found a way for them to stay and be happy despite the danger."

"By stripping away everything that makes them human," objected Sumi.

The Lady of the Dead raised an eyebrow. "You think only motion makes a human?"

"No," said Sumi sullenly. They were passing through a hall with domed, frosted glass windows covering the ceiling, turning the light into a gilded brightness that illuminated them all as if they had joined the ranks of the dead. The statues here were still intact, standing calm and elegant atop their plinths.

"Our statues work very hard to be able to do the things they do, and they take pride in their accomplishments," said the Lady. "Those who don't take that pride lose their certainty and return to the worlds of their birth in short order. They have friendships here, rivalries. They fall in love, and some take lovers in the slow hours of the night, when the halls are sleeping and the dead sleep with them. They move slowly, but they do move, and their passions can burn as hot as they do in any other world. We steal nothing of their humanity. We merely give them other avenues for expressing it."

Sumi frowned deeply, looking toward Nancy. Nancy met her eyes and nodded, agreeing with the Lady.

"But . . . I can understand people going away from their friends when they're doing it to *do* something," protested Sumi. "If they're being a mermaid or operating a shop or taking off their skin so they can marry their one true love. I don't understand doing it just to do nothing forever."

"Standing still isn't doing nothing," said the Lady. "I think that's where you're confusing who *you* are as a person with who my statues are. They're all different, and they all have their reasons for being here, but none of them are less of a person or less human than you are, except for the ones who were never human in the first place. Your world isn't the only one whose doors can lead a person here."

Sumi nodded, still frowning, and continued their trek in silence.

At the end of the hall was a ballroom, large and elegant and echoingly empty. On the other side of the ballroom was a study, small and elegant and almost rustic in its design, with a fire burning in the fireplace and no one there to greet them. And on the other side of the study was a library, shelves of books reaching upward into eternity.

In that library stood a tall, thin man with skin the color of ash and hair the color of bone. His eyes were pale, almost silver in their lack of color, and he was holding a book in one long-fingered hand. He raised his head at the sound of footsteps, a small smile appearing on his lips when he saw the Lady.

"I feared it was another contingent of the statuary come to request a passage to another place," he said.

This time, it was Christopher who frowned. "I thought that as soon as our certainty wavered, we would be popped right back out into our own worlds. At least that's the way it's worked for most of us."

"Not wanting to die is not the same thing as being unsure, little skeleton," said the Lord. "Not wanting to die is the natural state of all living things. They come to Me seeking survival, not exile, and when I can, I grant it to them. Some will be lost to us forever, but others will find a way back. Their certainty will guide them."

"Ah," said Christopher.

"But no, you found Our Nancy, and her friends, and perhaps they can find the answer to what plagues Us." The Lord of the Dead placed a bookmark in the book, saving his place, and closed it, sliding the book back onto the shelf before turning his full attention toward Nancy. "What have you learned?"

"We've learned that the ghosts are being rallied by one spirit, a girl named Jill Wolcott, originally from the world most of us first came from, later of the Moors."

The Lord of the Dead scowled. "I should have known the Moors were involved! Terrible, untidy place that they are. They've never been content to allow the laws of nature to stand unchallenged there, and their disrespect spills out into everything around them. She must have been pulled here upon her death, and, once she had remembered herself sufficiently, began her campaign of destruction. What are you going to do about it?"

Nancy flinched. "We're going to do whatever we can to help, but we don't have your power, sir," she said. "Sumi can see the ghosts. Christopher can control their movements—to a degree—but we don't know the limits of what he can do, and I'd rather not find out by *dying*. Kade can—"

"I can give Jill a stern talking-to, but that isn't going to save your world," said Kade. "I don't know what is."

"If you can lead her and her army back to the room where the unquiet dead are meant to wait, I can seal the door behind them," said the Lord of the Dead. "Think of it as a parade, child of Mariposa. You favor parades there, do you not?"

"We do," said Christopher.

"What about me?" asked Talia. "What can I do?"

"The ghosts attacked your moths," said Sumi. "How many do you think you can control at one time?"

Talia shrugged. "How many have you got?" she asked.

Sumi grinned.

A DOOR AT THE BACK of the library opened onto the grounds, letting Talia and Sumi exit into a stretch of garden they hadn't seen before. In the distance, the treetops of the pomegranate grove scraped against the sky.

"How close do you need to be?" asked Sumi. "Can you call them from here?"

Talia frowned thoughtfully, looking toward the trees. Then she stopped and spread her arms, chin tilted very slightly toward the sky. She waited that way for several seconds.

Nothing happened.

"Nope," said Talia, dropping her arms.

"Great, so we keep going," said Sumi, and skipped gamely on.

Talia followed, working hard to keep up with Sumi as they crossed the vast expanse of green. "Was coming along on this a good idea?" she asked.

Sumi shot her a withering look. "No, of course not," she said. "But I'm glad you did, now that it looks like we're going to need millions of moths to lure the dead back to their room."

"I don't know that I like the idea of using my moths as bait," said Talia.

"Why not?"

"They're living things; they didn't agree to be a part of all this. They should be allowed to go about the business of being moths, without needing to save a bunch of people they don't know. Did you know that some species of moth don't even have mouths after they come out of their cocoons? They eat so much as caterpillars because after they get their wings, they starve to death. They just exist to mate and die, but they get to fly first, and that's enough for them."

"Huh," said Sumi. "Did you like moths this much before you went to Mothland?"

"I'm going to assume you mean Yuemingyuan, and you don't understand how offensive you're being, so there's no point in getting mad at you for it."

"Sure," said Sumi. "Go with that."

Talia shot her a confused sidelong look. "What?"

"If you have an assumption, you should go with it, especially when it makes me look better than I actually am." Sumi shrugged. "It's easier for me if we just let you be right all the time, about everything. I am a shallow, candy-colored pixie flitting through the world, doing nothing of weight or meaning."

Talia glared at her. "I didn't say that."

"You didn't need to say that." Sumi shrugged. "I am what I am, as you are what you are. If my travels left me a little scattered, and yours left you inclined to count everything off like it was going to be a structured poem, who's to say which one of us is right? We come from different styles of story. We have incompatible genres. Did you like moths before your Door?"

"I did," said Talia, still sounding baffled. "They're pretty, like butterflies but without the good PR. They fly around in the dark, and they're so fascinating and special. I used to feel like I'd won something every time I saw a moth. Then I went to a world where everything was built around moths—or to a culture, anyway. Yuemingyuan was the size of a whole planet, and my people weren't the only ones living there. Just the ones who mattered to me. The ones who were my family."

"Huh," said Sumi. "Confection isn't like that. Confection is a world that someone made, baked layer by layer over eons of time, and we don't really have that much cultural variation. All the people in Confection came through Doors from other worlds in the beginning, and the Baker made them candy hearts so they could stay and be happy and thrive in a place where there's only sugar, not get sick from malnutrition and go as dead as last season's gingerbread. But my world is all them, and their children, and their children's children. We didn't displace anyone because there was no one to displace, and when we needed a new continent, we just asked the world for it and watched it grow out of the ovens."

"Wow," said Talia. "That sounds . . . Oh, who am I kidding. That sounds absolutely awful."

"That's why Confection didn't call you," said Sumi. "I don't think I would like to go to where everything is moths and rules. It wouldn't make me happy."

"And I don't think I'd like to go where everything is all new and all the same," said Talia. "I like traditions. I like histories so heavy you can feel them in your hands, and so long and light you can wrap them around you like a cloak."

"So I guess you must like it here."

"Not really." Talia glanced around, looking suddenly uneasy. "There's weight here, but it's old and cold and doesn't bend itself toward kindness. Who looks at a problem like 'The dead are killing our guests' and decides that the answer is a worldwide game of freeze tag with fatal consequences for the losers? It's just not . . . it's not kind. The Great Song wouldn't have any room for this verse."

"Huh." They were almost to the garden wall, which was tall and strong with no visible breaks. Sumi turned around, walking backward so she could face Talia as they continued walking. "Why is your world's name in Chinese? I've only ever heard you speak English. We hear the names of our worlds in languages we can understand. That's why mine is Confection. I only know English well enough for it to matter. My parents always hated that I didn't want to learn Japanese."

"My great-grandmother went through a magical door when she was just a little girl in China," said Talia. "She told me the world she traveled to was called Yuemingyuan—the Garden of Moonlight—and that's where I went, too." Her face crumpled. "I wasn't sure enough because I wanted to make it back in time to tell her that I'd learned how to sing the Great Song, and that the verses she'd added were still there, that they remembered her. So I wasn't sure I wanted to stay. And then I made it back, and she'd died while I was traveling, and I didn't get to tell her after all."

"It's all right," said Sumi. "If you'd been able to be sure enough to stay, part of you would always be wondering what she would have said when you told her. The not-knowing would have eaten you away inside like acid, and then you'd have been all rotted through and breakable. This is better. This is just for now. Someday you'll make it back to Yuemingyuan, and all of this will be forgotten."

Talia nodded, eyes wide and awed.

Sumi smiled at her, gesturing to the wall, which was close enough to reach out and touch. "Go ahead. Call the moths."

Talia nodded again, spreading her arms, and hummed a single soft, low note.

And the moths came, Sumi laughing in delight the whole time, as the air turned into a shower of brown and orange wings, blotting out the world, blotting out the sun. Talia hummed, and the moths came, and everything was beautiful.

10 BATTLE PLANS

TALIA AND SUMI RETURNED to the library absolutely covered in moths, which had landed on them like gowns of autumn leaves, occasionally dotted with spots of blazing fire as the individual moths opened and closed their wings. More moths fluttered along behind them, dispersing themselves around the library to land on shelves, books, and the other occupants.

The Lady of the Dead looked with delight at a moth that had landed on her outstretched hand, lifting it to the level of her eyes so she could study it more closely. "Oh, these are marvelous," she said. "Where did you find them?"

"In the pomegranate groves," said Talia. "They're fruit-sucking moths. They have a specialized probiscis that can pierce the skin of the fruit and let them get at the juice. But that leaves holes in the rind, and bacteria and other pests can get in that way. They destroy what they need to survive."

"I thought you said moths starve," said Sumi.

"*Some* moths starve," said Talia. "These ones are more about starving other people. They can ruin a whole crop if you let them. And they're beautiful, which makes it harder for a lot of people to just squish them."

"There's no need to squish them when we have a whole army of hungry ghosts to feed them to," said Nancy, sounding uneasy. "Is this really going to work?"

"The ghosts go after life and movement," said Kade. "They

took the moths first before, and it's not like we can tell them to hold still if they don't want to be haunted to death."

"Moths spend a lot of time holding still," said Talia.

"That's not the point," said Kade. "They're moths. They'll fly whether we want them to or not, and if they're moving and alive, the ghosts will take them before they take the statues. It should work."

"I love the word 'should' in there," said Christopher dryly. "It's definitely not doing all the heavy lifting when you're asking me to risk myself."

"We're all at risk here," said Nancy.

"Are we?" Christopher looked to the Lord of the Dead. "Because it feels like to me that the two people who started this whole statuary system are probably not in any real danger."

"A mere ghost could not consume Me," said the Lord of the Dead. "They would break their teeth to even try."

"So why haven't you been out there drawing fire for your statues?" asked Christopher sharply. "If you could distract the dead, why wouldn't you?"

"I am the Lord of this place," said the Lord of the Dead. "I have other matters to attend upon."

"I think he's scared that maybe he's not as impossible to eat as he thinks he is," said Sumi. "Even a jawbreaker cracks eventually. Maybe all the ghosts working at one would be able to get to the Tootsie Roll center of the eldritch being."

They all turned to look at the Lord of the Dead, some of them more thoughtfully than others. Nancy, who had a moth perching on the tip of her nose, looked sad.

"Sir?" she asked. "Why . . . ?"

"Oh, Nancy," he said, sighing. "You were a favorite of Mine when you first came here. You learned Our ways so quickly, held yourself so beautifully still, and found new poses to bend your limbs against, like you were a sculptor in your own right, and your body made of finest marble. I was so sorry when you had to go, but I saw in you the potential to be a true work of art. It wouldn't have been fair to keep you before you were ready."

Nancy said nothing, just frowned and watched him with shadowed eyes.

"But since your return, you've been willful and obstinate. You don't listen as I expect one of My statues to listen. I've seen you adjust yourself in the middle of the day, long before the nightly bells grant their permission. And now I wonder—are you rebelling? Do you need to be released from Our service?"

Nancy gasped. The Lady of the Dead scowled, rounding on her husband.

"She left her world for Us," she snapped. "She risked her life to return there and find help, even knowing that she might not be able to find her way back again, or quickly enough to save the people she was worried about. She has served nothing but well, and You would question her because she dared to question You? We've never had rules against the statues questioning Us. We never wanted them. 'We're not gods,' remember? That was what You told Me when You first brought Me here, to Your halls, to walk with You. When I was only a wandering child from another world entirely, You told Me We were not gods, only the people who would anchor an empty world against the void, who would fill more of the universe with light and purpose. I have indulged the dead. I have followed the rules of Our world as it formed around Us, and I have never questioned why that world works so constantly to devour itself. Perhaps I should be questioning more. Perhaps I should be questioning You."

The Lord of the Dead shot her a stricken look. "My love, she is only a statue."

"Half Our subjects are 'only statues.' We owe them better than We are showing them now."

He sighed heavily and turned to Christopher. "Why have I not attracted the dead with My own flesh to spare the weaker? Because the candy girl is correct. I don't know how many would break themselves against Me before they began making headway, before they could chew through My skin to the bone beyond. I was only a man when I found this place, and I have grown to something near godhood as a grain of sand can grow into a pearl."

"That's actually a pretty common misconception," said Talia. "Pearls happen around any sort of irritant, usually caused by injury or the presence of parasitism. Sand is a relatively rare trigger for the process . . ." She gradually trailed off, noticing how many people were looking at her, and her cheeks flushed red. "But that wasn't the point. It works as a metaphor, I guess."

"Thank you for the approval," said the Lord of the Dead dryly. "Regardless, I do fear that the dead might devour Me if given the opportunity to try, and this world needs Me to keep it working as it does."

"Not every world has a genius loci, but the ones that have them need to keep them if they want to stay the way they are," said the Lady of the Dead.

"Like our Baker?" asked Sumi.

"Or our Scribe?" asked Talia.

The Lady nodded. "Without knowing them, I assume the answer. Yes. So My Lord husband avoids the danger for the sake of the world, and I . . . I have been lax in My duty of service. I should have sheltered more of Our residents, not only helped them to escape. This is their home as much as it is Ours. More, in some ways, because they have chosen it recently enough to continue choosing with every dawning day."

"What do you mean?" asked Kade.

"I mean that once a choice has been made for long enough, it is a choice no longer," said the Lady. "The door that might have taken Me back to My beginnings, had I chosen to leave this place for any reason, closed itself many years ago. The world that was is now no longer, and I have nowhere else to go."

There was something unutterably sad about the idea of someone's original home being lost that completely, even if it wasn't home anymore. For a moment, silence claimed the room, filling it with melancholy. Kade was the first to turn toward the door.

"We have a plan," he said. "We leave here with the moths, and Talia keeps them with us until the dead show up. Sumi can tell us when the ghosts are coming. As soon as they arrive, Christopher begins playing them into a line, and Nancy leads us to the room where they're meant to stay. They can eat the moths to keep themselves calm and away from any statues we pass. Does that sound right to everyone else?"

"It does," said Nancy.

"I am incredibly unhappy about this plan, but yes, that sounds about right," said Christopher. "I'll do my best to keep the invisible army from eating us all."

"I believe in you," chirped Sumi. "But one question, still. How are we supposed to keep them inside the room once we get them there? Christopher can't just stand outside playing his flute forever, and if we stop and try to walk away, the ghosts are just gonna come out and swallow us all up like bonbons."

The Lord and Lady of the Dead exchanged an unhappy look.

"We thought you would know," they said.

Sumi stomped her foot. "I'm resurrected but that doesn't mean I know everything! If resurrected people knew everything, Jill would have been smart enough not to steal her sister's body in the first place! She'd have known it was never going to work."

"You're not resurrected," said the Lord of the Dead. "I look at you and I don't see a prior death."

Sumi looked poleaxed, turning to stare almost accusingly at Kade, who put his hands up defensively.

"Hey, don't look at me in that tone of voice," he said. "I was part of the little clown parade that brought you back. You were deader'n a doornail when we started out."

"But we didn't *resurrect* her," said Christopher, voice slow and thoughtful. "That implies using the body you've already got. We just took the pieces of her that still existed to the Baker, and got her a whole new body. She's the Sumi of Theseus."

"So we could offer to make Jill a whole new body to move into?" asked Sumi. "I know I'm not always the best at predicting consequences, but that sounds like a real bad idea to me. I'm pretty sure Jack would kill us all for even thinking about it too long."

"Do you have salt here?" asked Kade, returning his attention to the Lady. "Salt can work pretty good at keeping ghosts back. On Prism we mostly used crystals, and we only needed those in certain areas, but I've heard good things about salt."

"As have We, which is why We don't keep very much on hand," said the Lord of the Dead. "The dead belong here. We've never needed to seal doors against them before."

"Why don't we ask Nadya?" asked Sumi abruptly. "I remember you said she came with you when you came here to get me back, and she stayed behind. Well, Nadya's a Drowned Girl. Her whole door was about water. There's salt in water. I bet Nadya would know how to get salt *out* of the water."

The Lady of the Dead made a complicated face. "I'm sorry, but that won't be possible."

"Why not?" asked Kade.

"Your friend *did* remain here when the rest of you moved along, this is true," said the Lady of the Dead, in the halting tone of an adult telling children things they might not be happy to hear. "But she vanished only a few weeks later. We believe she returned to Belyyreka. That her willingness to stay here for the sake of your quest succeeding was enough to tell the doors that she was truly sure the world where she had been born was no fit home for her. At any rate, We found her tracks by the water, and no sign of her, either breathing or body, and it seems most likely that she was able to go home."

For a moment, everyone in the room stared at her, except for the Lord of the Dead, who had become suddenly very interested in the moth resting on his sleeve. Then, almost explosively, they all began to speak at once:

Nancy: "You didn't tell me she was missing! I thought she was just down by the water, and would come to see me when she got around to it! I would have—"

Christopher: "—looked for her? Or did you just go ho-hum, expendable teenager from another world, who gives a crap if she's drowned in our low-rent version of the River Styx? At the very least—"

Kade: "—you should have told us as soon as we got here. You had to know we'd ask about her eventually! Can you really expect us to save your world when you couldn't even save Nadya?"

Talia: "But I thought going back through our Doors was a good thing."

That was enough to stop the rest of them yelling. All save Sumi, who was just getting her thoughts back together:

"Part of why we came at all was to make sure Nadya was okay," she said. "We didn't want her getting ghost-gobbled, especially not when she wouldn't be here if not for me getting all murdered and stuff. Nancy knew that. You should have known that. It feels a little weird that you didn't say anything until just now, like you knew we wouldn't be as happy to help if we weren't going to save Nadya by doing it."

The Lord of the Dead looked away.

"But the statues who live here don't deserve to get eaten either, especially not when it's just because they don't have really obnoxious friends who can see dead people and talk to moths and stuff." Sumi shrugged. "So I guess we're doing this."

The Lord of the Dead looked back, staring at her. "You were always going to do this," he accused.

"Yup," said Sumi.

"Are you just being unpleasant because you can?"

"I think not enough people have been unpleasant to you in a very long time," said Sumi amiably. "You need to be reminded that sometimes it just sucks to suck. So you suck, sir. Congrats on that. Now take us where we need to go."

"I cannot—" he began, and paused as the Lady of the Dead lifted one eyebrow silently. He sighed. "I suppose I will walk you to the room of containment. We may not pass the dead along our way. If we don't, I will return here, and you will search for them."

"Translation: you'll get yourself to safety, and leave us to play the canaries in your coal mine," said Kade coldly. "Not very lordly of you, *sir.*"

"In this place, I set the rules of lordly behavior," said the Lord of the Dead. "I am terribly sorry not to live up to your vaunted standards."

"Oh, great, the boys are fighting," said Sumi with a layer of vicious delight.

"Let's go," said Christopher, and started for the door.

11 HAUNTS AND HAVENS

THE SILENCE IN THE HALLS had grown even deeper while they were removed from it. They left the library in a straight line, the Lord of the Dead at the front with Sumi close behind him, Christopher following her, and Kade following him. Talia came after Kade, surrounded and trailed by her vast cloud of moths. Nancy walked in the middle of that cloud, still stuttering like a stop-motion animation transplanted into the real world, but less now than ever. She was warming back up to normal human speeds, and soon enough the way she walked would be indistinguishable from the rest of them.

They walked past rank upon rank of living, frozen statues, and past even more empty plinths, some dusted with that same faint reddish-brown blood splatter, others fresh and clean and waiting for their next occupants. Sumi leaned forward.

"How many statues would you say you've got around here when things are normal?" she asked. "Ballpark figure."

"Twelve hundred or so, sometimes less, very rarely more," he said. "More than that and they become difficult to tend to with the staff We're able to maintain."

"Staff?" asked Christopher blankly.

"Not everyone who finds their way here holds the gift for stillness, but that doesn't mean they're ready or willing to return to the worlds of their birth," said the Lord of the Dead, haltingly. "When that happens, when they're willing to take the risk of the roving dead if it means they can stay here, in whatever safety this place represents to them . . . We train them to operate the kitchens and maintain the halls. Someone has to feed the statues, to help them down when the time comes for them to bathe and . . . do other things."

"Is the Lord of the Dead embarrassed by the word 'shit'?" asked Sumi, sounding oddly charmed. "What an old-fashioned little twitch!"

He shot her a venomous look, cheeks burning red. Sumi laughed it off.

"The staff makes sure the statues can live in peace and contentment," he continued. "And before you ask, there are four hundred or so of them, and they've all been moved to safety for the time being. My Lady and I have been seeing to the statuary on Our own."

For the first time, Kade looked almost impressed by something the Lord of the Dead had offered about the way his household functioned. He nodded, small and tight, and said, "That's as it should be, a man taking care of his people when he needs to."

"There are too many statues when things are as they're meant to be for Us to hide them all in our warded chambers. And wards sufficient to bar the dead take months to construct, blood and salt and silver and tears. We couldn't put them all behind walls of gossamer and glass in the time we had. The attacks began too suddenly."

"People in earthquake country don't normally build to protect themselves from hurricanes," said Sumi. "Story checks out."

They were approaching an intersection. Sumi motioned for the Lord of the Dead to pause for a moment, then crept forward, looking tensely down one corridor, and then the other. Then she relaxed, sagging slightly as the tension left her.

"No ghosts here," she said.

The procession continued on.

WHEN TALIA HAD FIRST fallen through the door in the back of her mother's study to a world filled with moonlight and the low, steady hum of a melody she already knew in her bones, she had been startled by the first whispers of moth-song, which was very different from human-song, or even the rabbit-song performed so joyfully in the next country over. Yuemingyuan had been a revelation that unfolded slowly as a flower, each petal presenting a new series of challenges and surprises, but sweetened the air all the more.

She'd never thought much about moths before that moment. She knew them from her biology classes, and from nights by the back porch light with a net; her great-grandmother had always been fond of the little creatures, telling her how the silkworm had transformed China, how the moon moth could carry her secrets for her if she wanted to share them, but the stories of one elderly relative hadn't been enough to make moths personally important to her.

Then she had found herself in Yuemingyuan, where the moths sang their own history of the world, even the ones who had no mouths—their song was in the fluttering of wings and the scraping of legs against one another, softer than cricket-song but no less sincerely part of the beauty of the night. Passing through that door had opened her ears to the moth-song, and now that she could hear it, she could never unhear it.

Their little group moved through the Halls of the Dead, and the air was cold and harsh against her skin, unforgiving in a way she didn't have proper words for, and she knew her companions were speaking, but she tuned them all out, ignoring them in favor of listening to the whisper of moth wings beating at that strange, unfriendly air. They sang their own psalms to the man at the front of the group, told their own tales of his kindness and his cruelty. He had planted the pomegranate groves, they whispered, had tended the trees with his own hands; the first seeds had been carried to him by a traveler from another world, far-off and forgotten, and the fruit that child had clutched so closely had been dusted with moth eggs, unseen travelers on their own journey into the unknown.

Under the care of the Lord of the Dead, the seeds had sprouted with incredible speed, had taken root and shot upward, becoming fruiting trees in a matter of weeks. And the unseen moths' eggs had hatched and sent their caterpillars creeping into the good green to feed and grow, becoming cocoons in time, becoming moths, and all the while safe in a world without predators, without pesticides. The fruit had been plentiful enough for them to have their fill and a harvest still be ready for the statues, and the Lord and his Lady had walked among the trees, and it had been beautiful in all ways.

Talia could have liked the version of the Lord of the Dead who lived in the moth-song, the kindly man who planted trees and carefully moved caterpillars from one branch to another when he encountered them, rather than smashing them or flicking them away. All the moths agreed that caterpillars weren't thinking beings, were only delivery vehicles for a hunger that would only be sated by the long sleep of silk and the changes it entailed. To be kind to a caterpillar was to show mercy to a future that was far from guaranteed. In the eyes of the moths, it was the greatest act a biped was capable of.

They knew why she had called them. She had told them, of course, had explained that she was asking for their help when that help might well mean they never saw their home again. Moths—even moths hatched and fed in the Halls of the Dead—were short-lived creatures. Their continuity was in the moth-song, in the verses and lyrics that would be passed from one pair of beating wings down to the next. She had promised them that when this was all over, she would return to the pomegranate groves and sing their verses of the Great Song to the rest of the eclipse, to guarantee their heroism would not be forgotten.

So she walked and they flew, and she listened to their song, and when she heard holes begin appearing in that song, she looked back over her shoulder, down the silent length of the corridor behind her, and saw that there were far fewer moths there than there had been in the beginning. Her eyes widened as she watched a few at the very rear of the cloud dissolve into nothingness.

"Nancy!" she shouted, and her voice was a whipcrack through the quiet, ripping it into pieces and throwing them wildly in all directions.

Nancy turned her face toward Talia, eyes wide and worried.

Talia waved her arms over her head, frantic, like she was trying to guide a small aircraft to a safe landing.

"Run!" she shouted. "Get ahead of the moths! They're right behind you!"

She was making enough noise that the others turned around, Sumi's own eyes going wide as she saw what was coming up behind Nancy. Already swearing steadily, she began pushing her way through the group, heading for her friend.

"Hold on, ghostie-girl," she said. "Just run and we'll protect you."

Confronted on the one hand by people telling her to run and her own body telling her to freeze if she wanted to be safe, Nancy did the thing she'd been working on doing for most of her life: she stopped dead where she was, freezing in mid-step. It wasn't merely holding still. It was something more profound, a cold freeze that seemed to settle over her like a concrete shell, stiffening and hardening her in place until she wasn't breathing, until her heart forgot to beat. She couldn't see the ghosts coming up behind her. She could hear them, though, a rushing like wind, even softer than the beating of the moths' wings.

But without her heartbeat echoing in her ears, Nancy could hear sounds fainter than should have been possible. She could hear the whispers of the dead within that wind, their hopes and their fears and their terror of the girl who led them, which should have been ridiculous—she was as dead as they were, she couldn't hurt them—but was somehow tragic instead. Some of the voices were familiar, the voices of her fellow statues, stripped of life and breath and the capacity for change, pressed flat as a butterfly under glass; others were strangers to her, the dead of other places, other stories. And they were all rushing in her direction, and she couldn't move. To move would be to admit that she was done with living.

She had never been done with living. For all her stillness, all her willingness to dream and drift her way through her days, she was *alive*, and she had always wanted to stay that way. Dreams were for the living, after all, and she enjoyed her dreams too much to give them up so easily. The whispers of the dead drew closer, drowning out Sumi's shouts, obscuring the sound of wings.

Then she was surrounded. The air around her grew cold, and it was only her years of learning to control her body's every reaction that allowed her to stop the autonomic reactions to the chill. Through extreme focus, she tamped down the gooseflesh that wanted to erupt along her arms, forced the hair on the back of her neck to remain flat and motionless.

The wind brushed against her exposed shoulders, feeling like the fingers of a cold, cold hand. In her ear, Jill's voice whispered, "You can stand still. Oh, I'm so very impressed. This isn't a game of freeze tag, little statue: you don't win if you just wait us out. You lose as soon as you need to take a breath. I know you statues still breathe. You have an hour at most before your body betrays you and you move again."

The wind swirled around Nancy, drowning out every other sound in the world, and she was going to die. It was as simple and straightforward as that. She was going to die, and there was nothing she could do about it.

She couldn't even close her eyes.

All she could do was wait.

FOR SUMI, WATCHING THE DEAD surround Nancy was something out of a horror movie, heartbreaking and impossible. They were less figures than they were the impressions of figures, white chalk sketches of faces and reaching hands somehow drawn in open air, like thin fog that clutched and caught. They ruffled Nancy's hair and clothing, setting them swaying, and that looked enough like motion that Sumi's own breath caught in her throat, choking her.

"Christopher," she said, in a completely reasonable tone, not raising her voice at all, "I need you to start playing your flute now."

Christopher, who had been standing frozen since Talia

shouted, lifted his flute to his lips and blew, beginning to move his fingers across the depressions. None of them could hear the music he played, not even the Lord of the Dead, but they could feel it, like an impending storm hanging in the air.

He walked slowly forward as he played, moving toward the stationary Nancy and her entourage of the unfriendly dead, playing all the while. Sumi nodded, looking relieved.

"They're lining up," she said. "Move them away from Nancy if you can. Try and get her clear. She's not going to move, so the dead will need to. Play faster."

Christopher nodded, fingers moving faster as he picked up the tempo. Talia whistled silently, and the moths flocked to flutter enticingly between her and Nancy. A few of them came apart as the grasping hands of the dead reached out and snatched at them, reducing them to dust and dreams. Talia winced, but didn't call her moths away.

As the silver motes of light appeared and swirled, some of them floated closer, stopping just shy of Talia and coming together to form the pale outline of the fair-haired girl in the long, lacy gown. She smirked at the group.

"Decided to come crawling back and throw yourselves upon my mercy?" she asked. "Thanks for bringing us the snacks. They help to take the edge off." She reached out with one translucent hand, plucking a moth out of the air. She popped it into her mouth and bit down, and the moth came apart like all the others, dissolving into the substance of her. Another silvery mote joined her outline, which already looked more solid than it had been the first time they saw her.

Jill swallowed, and smirked again, watching the others. "My demands are simple. Take me back to the Moors, bring me back to life, and I'll call off my army. Leave me dead, and all your pretty knickknacks can join me on this side of the grave. It's your choice."

"We don't have a way of getting to the Moors from here," said Kade. "Jill, please. Be sensible. You're smarter than this. You know the Doors don't open on demand."

"That sounds like a you problem," said Jill. "It and I have that in common. Right now I'm also a you problem. And I've offered you a solution. Take it or don't—it's your call either way."

"I am the Lord of these Halls," said the Lord of the Dead, pushing his way through the group to glare at Jill. "You will stop this misbehavior at once, and return to your confinement."

"Oh, the big, strong man wants me to go and be a good little girl and sit in my room while he does *fucking nothing* to make things better for us," said Jill. "You pamper your little living statues and you ignore the dead who supposedly own this place. You don't help us find our passage on to the next life we're meant for, or offer us ways to return to the lives we had, that were cut short too soon. You're *useless*, lord-man. I've seen a *true* lord. I've served under him. He's tasted the sweetness of my blood, which is more than you can say you've ever done."

"I do not drink the blood of shades," said the Lord, sounding disgusted. "It's no better than sour wine, tainting the tongue and curdling the belly. The lord you claim to serve would not have you if you came before him now."

For a moment, Jill's face distorted into rage, transparent skin drawing so tight across her bones that she became nothing more than a grinning skull, sharp and terrible. Her eyes sank into her head, blackened pits through which could be seen nothing of any value.

Then she shook her rage away, returning to the appearance of a pretty, dainty young girl. "He wouldn't, no," she said. "My lord doesn't traffic in the true dead. He prefers the undead, who still walk in flesh and fear the sun. But restore my body and he'll love me again. Reset the lines between the living and the dead, and let me go home."

The longing in her last word was painful. Sumi winced.

"I didn't like being dead either, Jill," she said. "It was boring and it was lonely and it was cold. And it's not fair that I got to come back when so many others don't. But I got to come back because people cared about me enough to try. No one cares that much about you. Your own *sister* is the one who killed you—because you tried to kill her first. You deserve everything that's happening to you right now, and I'm not going to get in the way of you getting what you deserve."

"Sumi," hissed Kade. "Why are you antagonizing the nasty dead girl?"

"I don't like it when she's all calm and awful," said Sumi. "She doesn't deserve to be calm and awful. She's been killing people, and she needs to stop killing people, so I'm going to be nasty to her if I want to be."

Jill glared at her, clearly seething. "You take that back," she snapped.

"Nope," said Sumi.

"Take it back or I'll make you sorry," she said.

"How are you going to make me sorry?" asked Sumi. "You're *dead*."

"'Dead' only means as much as you let it mean," said Jill hotly. She surged forward—or tried to, anyway. Christopher blew harder into his silent flute, fingers moving faster and faster. Jill seemed to hit an invisible barrier between her and Sumi, and shrieked, thrashing against it like a bug slamming up against a windscreen. She pulled back again, shooting Christopher a look filled with pure, burning loathing.

"I'll remember this, bone-boy," she snapped, and vanished, bursting into silver motes.

They swirled through the air, moving away from the group to rejoin the dead clustered around Nancy. The motes drew tight, covering her in a net of glimmering brightness, then raced off down the hall, dragging the motionless Nancy with them.

Kade shouted and threw out his hand like he was going to grab hold of her. Christopher stopped playing to grab him, holding him back. The silver lights winked out, and Nancy was gone.

12 WHAT WE OWE THE DEAD

SILENCE FOLLOWED NANCY'S disappearance. Kade turned, with aching stillness, to look at Christopher, who shied away.

"You want to tell me *why* you decided to do that?" he asked, in a low, dangerous voice.

"They can't hurt her unless she moves," said Christopher frantically. "She's safer than any of the rest of us would be."

"They'd have taken you all the way apart," said Sumi. "No more Kade, no more voice of reason, and then where would the rest of us be? Would we have to find our own ways to be reasonable? Because I don't think we know how to do that anymore. You've been so good at being reasonable for the rest of us for so long that we don't know how to be reasonable without you, and we'd all get dead, and then we'd be stuck with stupid ghost Jill all up in our faces all the time, being all wispy and awful. Or maybe she'd be able to boss us around the way she can all the other ghosts in this place, and then we'd be a part of her ghost army, and that would be *awful.* I don't want Jill to be the boss of me."

Kade turned to scowl at her, and Sumi looked unflinchingly back. He turned his attention on Talia, who flinched.

"What?" she demanded. "I let the ghosts eat a whole bunch of my moths! I didn't stop you from getting to the statue-girl! I haven't done anything wrong here!"

Kade held his scowl for a long moment, then sighed and

sagged. "I guess you haven't," he said. "But what are we supposed to do now?"

THE DEAD SURROUNDED NANCY, digging their fingers into her hair and locking them around the draped lines of her chitoniskos, and they pulled her down the hall before she could do anything to stop them. Not that there was anything to have been done: from her position, she would have been devoured in an instant if she had tried to break away and run from them. They had her, and she knew they had her, and so when they hauled her away, she remained as perfectly immobile as stone, not allowing her eyes to water or her heart to beat.

It was a difficult thing, to be so still that her body forgot what it was to be a body, and began to learn what it was to be a thing. She couldn't maintain it for too long. The oldest statues warned about that, whenever someone chose to stay and stand; they told the new statuary that to be too still was to risk losing the self, to become as inanimate as they aspired to be. To freeze so completely that the body calcified was a terrible way to die, and there was no coming back from it.

Sooner or later, to stay alive, she would have to breathe. And as soon as she did, the dead would be able to consume her. So she held her position as they dragged her down the hall, and she hoped against all odds that her friends would be able to find a way to come and take her back before it was too late.

At the end of the hall was a door, one that she had seen frequently during her time in the Halls, but had never passed beyond. It was a sweeping filigree of gold, burnished bright and glowing like the sun. It swung open as the dead dragged her toward it, and they pushed her into the darkness beyond.

In an instant, Nancy was stranded in the infinite black of the void at the beginning of eternity, the blackness that existed before the birth of light, when all the worlds were yet to be and could not yet be reached. There were no doors here, because this was the place past which no light could shine.

This was a space sliced out of the crucible in which stars were born and pushed out into the universe to find their way, the beginning of everything, and there was no light there, there was no warmth or oxygen, only the dark emptiness of infinity. Her heart clenched in her chest, and she felt it contract, almost moaning with the realization that her concentration had failed: she was finished, she was done, the dead would have her now.

But the dead did not descend, and Nancy did not die.

Instead, she allowed her harried heart to beat, and let her lungs fill with the taste of newborn stars and acrid ashes, and she didn't know how she could be alive here, and she didn't know how long it was going to last, but she knew she wasn't going to waste the time she had. She wrapped her arms around herself, seeking some comfort in the contact with her own skin, and bit by bit, she shivered and sank into the void, sitting on the nothingness and waiting for the end to come.

Instead, a hand touched her shoulder, and she looked up to behold the faintly glowing shape of Jillian Wolcott, still silvered, but now tinted almost like she'd been when she was alive. She smiled, red, red lips bending upward in a liar's bow, and asked, "Mind if I sit?"

Nancy tried to scramble backward but could find no purchase on the void, so that her hands and heels only scrabbled. Jill laughed.

"You can't do anything here unless we allow it, Nancy.

You're our prisoner for the time being, and you get to decide how pleasant or terrible that's going to be."

"You said you were going to devour me," said Nancy.

"Oh, Nancy, Nancy," Jill chided. "I would love to devour you. I want to taste your heart between my teeth. I think you would be so much sweeter than you realize. But there's something I want even more than that."

"What?" asked Nancy blankly.

Jill managed, with a visible effort, not to laugh. "I want what you have, what you've been so patently determined to throw away like it doesn't mean anything at all. I want to *live*. I was so young, and so innocent, and I didn't deserve what happened to me."

Nancy stared at Jill, remembering her with hands gloved in blood and splatters on her pale gown. "You were never innocent," she said.

"But I was, once," Jill countered. "It's not my fault that I fell into bad company, and they made a monster out of me. I had my whole life in front of me. I could have been better than I ever had the chance to be, but they took that chance away from me."

"You took all Loriel's chances away from her," said Nancy. "And Sumi's. And Lundy's. They deserved better than what you did to them. No one forced you, Jill. No one put the knife in your hand or told you that you should use it. You did that all on your own. I don't know how you died, but I know how Sumi came back. She got a second chance because people loved her enough to come here and ransom her back from death—she was wanted. That's more than I can say for you."

Jill's hand caught her across her cheek and by surprise at the same time. Her head snapped to the side, and as she turned slowly back to face the other girl, she raised her own hand to touch her stinging skin with careful fingertips, staring.

"You *hit* me," she accused.

"I'll hit you again," said Jill. "I'd do worse, but we need you alive for right now. A dead hostage is about the most worthless thing there is. Although maybe they'd just bring you back, too. What do you think, fancy Nancy? Are you important enough to them that they'd go to all that trouble to have you back with them?"

Slowly, deliberately, Nancy closed her eyes and turned her face away.

A moment later, she heard fingers being snapped in front of her nose. She didn't react, forcing herself to remain rigidly still.

"Nancy," said Jill. "Nancy, do you really think ignoring me makes this go any better for you? Do you think it gets you a happy ending? I have you in the void at the beginning of time. There's no getting away from me here. There's no running. All ignoring me buys you is a little less grace when the time arrives."

Nancy didn't respond. Jill made a frustrated huffing noise and was silent. In time, Nancy began to believe that the other girl had in fact gone away; she relaxed where she sat, keeping her eyes closed. They were in the abyss that came before anything else existed. It wasn't like there was much for her to see.

PART III

AN UNQUIET GRAVE

13 A GIFT OF STARLIGHT

THE FIVE OF THEM WALKED through the halls, two boys, two girls, and a Lord of the Dead, all of them trailed by a full eclipse of moths. Some of the windows they passed were open, and more moths came drifting through those windows to join the cloud that ebbed and flowed around the taller of the two girls, often landing on the shiny black cap of her hair, wings fanning as she walked on.

None of the five said a word as they walked. They watched the world around them with grim focus, clearly following some unseen trail. The Lord walked at the front, and he set the path the rest of them would follow, marking every step with serenity and silence.

"What are we going to do?" asked the darker of the two boys, after they had gone so long in silence that it had become almost physical, a cruel sixth member of their company. "How are we going to get Nancy back from a bunch of hostile ghosts? How do we know she's even still there for us to recover?"

"We don't," said the second boy. "But she wouldn't give up on us, and we're not giving up on her. That's not how friends behave."

"She did give up on us once," said the first boy. "As soon as she saw her door, she was off and running, and she never did look back."

"And you can criticize her for that just as soon as you can convince me that you would have done any differently."

"There's no sense in fighting," said the Lord of the Dead, turning to face the others. "All of you know what's at stake here."

"But what we don't know is where we're going," said the shorter girl. "If you could tell us that, maybe we'd be less grumpy about the whole thing."

"Grumpy."

"Yes. We're irritated and antagonistic and sad. I think the emotion that makes is grumpiness, don't you?"

The Lord of the Dead shook his head. "You Nonsense children are exhausting. As to where we're going, I don't have an easy means of tracking the unquiet dead through the halls. If I did, I'd have been doing it all along, and we wouldn't have any need of this procession. But I know where the graceful dead are waiting, the ones who're content to wait for their rebirth to arrive."

"What do they have to do with this?" asked the girl with the moths.

"Sometimes when you're trying to fight an unstoppable force, the best answer is an immovable object," said the Lord of the Dead. "Sumi can see them. *I* can see them. Together, perhaps we can convince them that they should help."

"Fight ghosts with ghosts," said the first boy thoughtfully. "It's a terrible idea, but it's what we've got."

"I'm so glad you approve." They walked on, passing motionless statues and empty plinths, until they reached a door of silver filigree. It swung open at the Lord's touch, revealing an expanse of velvet darkness, treacle-thick and all-consuming. The Lord of the Dead stepped through into the abyss, which held him up as if it were solid ground. His flesh glowed a faint and lambent silver against the black, like a paler, more vital mirror of Jill's spectral form.

The four teens followed him, the moths accompanying them. All their living bodies glowed in the dark in the same fashion, even the moths, which darted back and forth, leaving glittering contrails behind themselves.

"Stay close," he said. "If I lose you in here, I'm not certain I can have you back again."

They didn't need to be told twice, but clustered close, Sumi going so far as to link her arm though his, like they were buddies going for a pleasant stroll. He looked down at her and she beamed up at him, giving his arm a squeeze.

"Take us to your grand solution," she said. "I want my ghostie-girl back again."

"She's My ghostie-girl, as you call her," he said, looking sternly down at her. "She chose My Halls, and My service, over you."

"We'll see," said Sumi, and said no more of that, turning her attention instead to scanning the dark around them for signs of motion.

At first there was nothing, only the dark, comfortable and all-consuming. For Christopher, Kade, and Talia, the nothing remained. For Sumi and the Lord of the Dead, specks of light began appearing, glowing softly silver in the distance. Sumi laughed and let go of his arm, stepping back a bit and spreading her own arms in welcome.

Dots of light began flocking out of the dark and covering her, plastering themselves to her skin like raindrops striking a solid object in their descent. She closed her arms, embracing as much of the light as she could while it swirled around her, tears glistening in the corners of her eyes.

"I remember you, I remember, I remember," she said. "We

were all dead together, you and I, and it was soft and quiet and beautiful, and I remember you."

More lights appeared, joining their fellows in swirling around her, painting her in a silvery gleam brighter than her own light had originally been. Christopher gasped.

"The skeletons on Mariposa would glow that way when they pulled themselves together as the sun went down," he said. "When they came back to life."

"The dead here do not come back to life, unless they go somewhere else to find that spark of lightning and starlight," said the Lord of the Dead. "But they are made of the same stuff as the living, always. My beloved dead. I am come to you tonight not as a lord, but as a petitioner, for I need your help. All the Halls of the Dead need your help. The Lady needs your help. Will you protect your home?"

More specks of silver collected, gathering on Sumi's skin and swirling through the air. All of them could see the ghosts now, they had gathered so thickly around them; this was their place, and they had been called, and oh, they were ready to come.

The silver gathered more and more thickly, until it began to form the outline of a child, a girl no more than eight years old. Her hair was dark and pinned into a bun; her clothing was rough and hand-stitched, more suitable to a production of *Peter Pan* than a playground, and she had owl feathers braided into her hair. What color she might have had once was gone, all rendered in the silver glow, and she was watching them with calm, unblinking eyes.

Kade gasped. "Lundy?" he asked.

"I was," said the girl. "I'm here to wait for my rebirth. Which means I'm awaiting a door to the Goblin Market, for this time I'll begin there, and give fair value all my days, not cheat anyone by disappearing from their home and halls. As soon as that door opens, I'm gone."

"But you knew these people in life?" asked the Lord of the Dead.

"I did, which is why I've been chosen to speak for us today. On another day, another might have been the speaker; on another day, I might have continued to drift and dream, and wait for the hour of my redemption. What do you want?"

The Lord of the Dead blustered for a moment, looking shocked. "You would speak to Me so bluntly?"

"I would speak to you however it pleases me, for I am dead and have no need for the rules of etiquette that bind the living," said Lundy. "You're no lord of mine. I appreciate the shelter you've offered to me, but as your power comes from our proximity, fair value is answered without any false civilities. I'm under no obligation to grant you more civility."

The Lord of the Dead scowled.

Kade stepped forward. "Howdy, Lundy," he said. "I'd ask how you've been, but I think 'dead' is a pretty stable state."

She nodded. "It tends to be, yes. What's going on?"

"Jill's here."

Lundy frowned. "Jill Wolcott? Jack's sister?"

Privately, Kade thought that calling Jill "Jack's sister" as if that were the most important thing about her might be enough to kill her a second time, this time through pure rage. He didn't say that, only nodded and agreed, "Yes, that's the one."

"She killed me," said Lundy. "You know that, right? Jill was the one who killed me. I didn't have much of a life, but it was mine, and I wasn't finished with it yet. She had no right to take it away from me like it was nothing."

"You're not wrong," said Kade. "If it helps at all, Jack

killed her not all that long after, because of what she'd done to you and to Sumi."

"And she's here?"

"She is. Her ghost is, anyway. She's in with the other ghosts, the ones who aren't willing to just sit and wait for their rebirth to arrive. And she's got Nancy."

"Nancy . . . that's the one who'd traveled here before she came to the school, isn't it?"

"Yes. When the unquiet dead started killing living statues, Nancy came back to the school looking for help. So we came to help her. Please, will you help us?"

"How?" Lundy spread her transparent arms, indicating the void around them. "We're *dead*, Kade. Ghosts. We have no substance outside this room, and what we have here is a loan from the Lord of the Dead to make us more comfortable."

"Jill and her army only have as much substance as they do because they steal it from the living," said the Lord of the Dead.

"Well, how did they get the substance to do that in the first place?" Sumi demanded, sounding frustrated. "You can't keep changing the rules on us! Either they have enough substance that they can catch and devour people or they don't. Either they can do harm or they can't. You can't have it both ways at the same time."

"It's my fault," said a new voice. As a group, they turned, even Lundy, to see a pale, silver-outlined figure in a flowing chiton standing some feet away, his translucent hands folded gravely in front of himself, his head bowed. He was clearly one of the statues—or had been, because he was just as clearly dead.

"What do you mean, Iason?" asked Lundy. Then: "What did you do?"

"I loved a boy," said the shade. "He was tall and handsome and strong, and he came from a world all unfamiliar to me, but beautiful when he whispered of it in the middle of the night. He was sure he belonged here. He was so sure. But in the end, when he settled into stillness, it was too much for him. His heart stopped in the middle of the long afternoon—truly stopped, not just paused—and he fell. He didn't get back up."

"Love isn't forbidden among My statues," said the Lord.

"No," agreed the shade. "We were never told not to love. But stillness as we have to practice it is very hard on the body. The heart wants to beat, not hold itself in stasis. The lungs want to fill. He stilled himself, as he had been taught to, and it killed him. I was . . . I was so very angry that he should be snuffed out so easily. He was the fire by which I warmed myself. A world without him was very cold and very cruel and I wanted no part of it."

"What did you do?" asked Lundy again, voice harder this time.

The shade—Iason—raised his eyes and met hers. "I left my pedestal in the middle of the night, when the other statues slept and the halls were silent. I found the door of silver and the door of gold, and I listened at them both until I heard Aleksy's voice, like a whisper carried by a dream. I opened the door, and heard the unquiet dead on the other side. They whispered and hissed and slid over one another like snakes in the darkness, and when I slipped into their company and asked them to return him to me, they told me what to do. They asked for blood. They said that if I bled for them, we could be together again. I was foolish and in love and thought they meant my blood would somehow start his heart beating again, put the breath back into his body and bring him back to me. Instead . . ."

"Instead, you bled, and they came to feast," said the Lord of the Dead. His tone was very nearly gentle. "They took their fill, and when they were done, they took what was left of you."

"Yes," said Iason. "They drank me dry and then devoured my body, bones and all, and expelled me from their company. I died, and still we aren't together. Still, we wait in separate rooms for the rest of eternity to unfold. How is this fair? All that I wanted was to be with my love."

"And now we know," said the Lord of the Dead. "There's always enough life lost for one or two of the hungry dead to find enough substance to do harm. They feed on small things, like the moths, and they strengthen themselves, and they attack the statues. But for them to have such numbers, they needed to be strong from the beginning. They took the blood of a grieving boy and they spun it into teeth and claws with which to devour all they came across, and every statue they fell grants them more strength, more substance with which to take what they desire. It explains why this happened now, and not the moment your Jill found herself here."

"She's not *our* Jill," said Christopher. "Don't call her that. We don't want her any more than you do."

"Ownership doesn't matter," said Lundy. "What do you expect us to do? We're *dead*. Let us rest."

"After you help us stop the unquiet, I will let you rest as long as you like," said the Lord of the Dead.

"But how?"

"Their weakness is their strength. They have too much substance to pass through things as the dead would normally do," said the Lord of the Dead. "If you will all come with us to the door of gold and hold them back from doing further harm, I believe we can lock them inside."

"And Nancy?" asked Kade.

"We can fight the other ghosts long enough to let you snatch her back," said Lundy. "She was an odd one, that Nancy, but she deserved better than to die at Jill's hands. We all did."

"Then you'll come?"

The look Lundy shot the Lord of the Dead was sharp and unforgiving. "Not for you, we won't," she said. "You've been a poor regent since I got here. You leave us alone and keep to yourself, and things like this happen. But for Nancy, and for my students? Yes, I'll come. I'll bring the dead. We'll have a haunting."

"Thank you," said Sumi. "I'm sorry you're still dead. Dead was awful boring."

"Thank you, Sumi," said Lundy. She smiled, then disappeared. The other motes of light winked out at the same time, and the form of Iason dissolved into sparkling mist, fading away.

"We should go," said Talia, feeling the shift in the air. This place had never been intended for the living, but it had tolerated them for a time. That time was coming to an end.

The Lord of the Dead nodded and turned back toward the door, the others hurrying along with him. Even Talia's moths seemed to understand the urgency. They surrounded the girl in a dense cloud, wings flapping frantically as they rushed for the exit.

The darkness whispered around the group, but nothing reached out to grab them or stop them from escaping. They stepped back out into the Halls of the Dead, and Talia gasped softly as she saw her companions in the light.

They were all of them rimed in glimmering motes of silver, like starlight dusted across their skin. Christopher wiped his fingers across his wrist, and frowned a little as the glow remained unchanged.

"Are we radioactive now?" he asked. "Do I need to be worried about this?"

"No," said the Lord of the Dead, glancing back at the closed silver door behind them. "The ghosts have gilded you with starlight. They'll know who not to fight when the moment comes. It's a valuable gift, but it will fade with time."

"Cool. As long as I'm not going to glow in the dark forever, I'm cool with it," said Christopher. "So what do we do now? Do we just wait here until something happens?"

"Lundy said she and the peaceful dead would come," said Kade. "I trust Lundy to keep her word."

"She didn't say when, though," said Sumi.

"I don't think she needed to. She wants to save Nancy, if only because it's Jill who's doing the threatening. That means she'll follow after us. We don't know how much time Nancy has."

It was sound logic, or as sound as anything could possibly be when dealing with the dangers of the dead. Sumi nodded, then asked, "So where are we going?" and turned an expectant eye on the Lord of the Dead.

He sighed. "This way," he said, and started walking.

The others followed, draped in starlight, leaving the silver door behind.

14 WHERE THE LIVING MEET THE DEAD

THE GOLDEN DOOR WAS on the other side of the building, what felt like almost a mile's walk away from the silver door. It made sense, to a degree, to keep the two types of ghost as far apart as possible—if some of them wished only for peace and the time to prepare for their own rebirth, while others wanted to fight the living for the chance of a return to their former state, they wouldn't make good neighbors. Still, it was a long walk, and Sumi started to whine before they were even halfway to their destination.

"—and then I'm going to eat a sundae with six kinds of ice cream and four kinds of sprinkles," she was saying as they rounded a corner and saw the golden door waiting up ahead.

The Lord of the Dead didn't even try to conceal his relief. "We're here," he said.

"Too bad," said Talia. "I was hoping to hear more about Sumi's perfect sundae."

"I can keep going," said Sumi.

"Please don't," said the Lord of the Dead. "I am begging you."

Sumi smirked. "Okay," she said easily enough, and skipped onward toward the door.

Kade frowned. "What do we do now?"

"We open the doors, and we hope Lundy keeps her word," said the Lord of the Dead.

"I don't like the sound of that," said Christopher. "I'm really not in the mood to be taken apart today."

"No one's getting taken apart when we're this close to finishing this whole thing," said the Lord of the Dead. He strode toward the closed golden door, reaching out to push it gently inward. It swung open, revealing the endless void.

If the void behind the silver door had been warm and welcoming, this one was an endless scream, cold and terrible and filled with a chittering sound, like a thousand insects crawling across each other in the darkness. Flashes of light split the distance, the echoes of dying stars.

The Lord of the Dead stepped back from the door, clapping his hands. "We require your presence," he said. "I wish to speak with you."

The air flexed, visibly pulsing, and then the motes of light began to appear, coalescing into the transparent figure of Jill Wolcott. She looked at the group of them with triumphant loathing before turning her full attention on the Lord of the Dead, smiling a small and poisonous smile. She curtseyed.

"Thank you, my lord, for your kind acknowledgment of our cause," she said.

"I acknowledge nothing," he said. "You asked Me for consideration, and I have considered. You are the dead. You have nothing to offer Me, and these people didn't come here to ransom you, as they once came to ransom Sumiko. They came because a friend asked for their help—a friend you have now threatened. Return Nancy Whitman to us at once, unharmed, and I will not punish you for what you've done. You acted only according to your natures. You are the hungry dead, after all, and the dead desire to fill their throats with life. The statues you've killed are gone. There's no bringing them back. They've joined your company or gone to rest with the waiting dead, and either way, they won't be returned to us. You are to return to your space, and stay there, and hunt these halls no longer. When the time comes, you may pass from here into your next lives. That is all I offer you."

"Then I refuse your offer," said Jill. "I want what I deserve. I want my life back. I want to return to the Moors and taste the Moon on my tongue. I want what's mine by right."

"No," said the Lord of the Dead.

Jill screamed—a high-pitched banshee's wail—and flung herself at him. Before she could impact against his skin, Lundy was suddenly there, holding her back, hands wrapped around spectral wrists.

"No," echoed Lundy.

Jill snarled, and the battle was joined.

More ghosts poured through the golden door, and were met with the dead of Lundy's army, all of them swirling around one another in an angry cloud of flickering mist. Sumi inched forward.

The statue Iason who had started all of this met in the middle of the hall with the specter of another statue. They didn't fight. Instead, they wrapped their arms around each other and held fast, Iason pressing his face to the other figure's shoulder and sobbing, body shaking from the force of phantom tears. The fight went on around them, and neither seemed to notice, only clung to one another, lost in their grief.

Sumi kept inching toward the door, until she had reached it without being ripped apart, and stepped into the void. Kade and Christopher followed her, leaving Talia and the Lord of the Dead behind. Talia's moths swooped through the open door. On the other side, the moths took on the same pale glow as the rest of the living, and they darted through the births of stars like heralds of the worlds and lives yet to come, bright-winged and only strange because they had yet to be considered by an expanding universe.

"Ghostie-girl!" shouted Sumi. "*Nancy!*"

"So you do know my name," said a wan voice from out of the darkness.

The group rushed toward it, and there was Nancy, sitting on the void, hands tucked between her knees and legs drawn up close to her chest, like she was trying to make herself as small as it was possible to be without giving up her physical body altogether.

"Come on, Nan, get it together," said Christopher, grabbing hold of her arm and trying to pull her to her feet.

It was like trying to shift stone. There was no softness to her, no yielding. Kade looked at the scene in front of him and realized, with cold and growing horror, that she was barely glowing.

"Nancy . . ." he said.

She turned her head to look at him, moving just as slowly as she had been when she first stepped back into the school. Every bit of motion felt like it took infinitely long, unfolding by degrees.

"It's cold here, Kade," she said. "It's really, really cold."

"She's been in the void for too long," said the Lord of the Dead. "You can't linger here. I can barely linger here. I will get her."

He stepped forward then, brushing Christopher aside, and scooped Nancy from the void into his arms. When he turned back toward the exit, he was moving as quickly as he ever did, and he carried her quickly with him back out into the light.

The others followed, Talia's moths fanning out around them in a protective cloud. Some of them vanished from the edges, picked off by ghosts that had been defeated outside and were retreating into their stronghold.

Still the group kept moving, until they stepped back into the thickened air of the hall, the two ghost armies clashing against each other. Figures flickered in and out of focus, then blurred back into the foggy throng. Sumi smiled a little as she spotted the shade of Lundy yanking on Jill's hair, jerking her phantasmal face toward the floor.

The Lord of the Dead continued until he was clear of the cloud, then looked back at Lundy. "Can you finish this?" he asked.

Lundy nodded. She let go of Jill's hair, and her ghosts swirled around her, the quiet dead gathering in both numbers and strength. It was something of a relief to realize that they outnumbered the angry dead, not only because it meant they were all less likely to be devoured. Most of the denizens of the Halls of the Dead were content with what their presence meant: they might not have wanted to die, but they were willing to wait patiently for their rebirth, not spend their days devouring the living and their nights considering worse.

Most of the dead were at peace, and that meant the universe was still, in some ways, essentially kind.

Lundy roared into the stillness, and her army pressed forward, shoving the unquiet dead back through the open door into the void. The Lord of the Dead, his arms full of Nancy, cleared his throat. "Can someone close that door?" he asked.

Christopher was the first to move. He rushed forward, slamming the door on the darkness. Lundy drifted over to him, gathering as much substance as she could, until she was a shining outline of a woman who had looked like a little girl, who had died an unkind death but would have died a worse one had she lived, who still had regrets.

"If you ever meet another traveler to the Goblin Market, please, give them a message to deliver for me," she said. "Tell them to go to the Archivist—everyone knows who she is, everyone knows how to find her—and tell her that Lundy has been lost, that the girl she banished paid fair value in the end for her mistakes. Tell them to ask her to tell Moon that my story is over, truly ended, but my heart belongs to the Market, and when time allows, I'll come back there to be reborn. I'll pay my own way, and I'll never spread my wings again."

"I will," said Christopher.

"The door must be sealed," said the Lord of the Dead. "While the angry dead have enough substance to kidnap a statue, they have too much to pass through solid objects. A good seal will keep them where they are."

"That sounds like us," said Sumi to Talia, skipping over to the door. She peeled off the bracelet around her left wrist as she moved, popping it into her mouth and beginning to chew.

Kade made a face, revolted. "Sumi, have you been wearing a bracelet of used chewing gum this whole damn time?" he asked.

Sumi shrugged, unrepentant. "It wasn't *that* used," she said. "I wanted to save it." She stuffed more bracelet into her mouth, chewing harder and harder as the gum reached choking density.

Finally, she pulled the gum out of her mouth and began stretching it out, before packing it along the bottom of the door. It still smelled faintly of strawberry. Kade turned away, clearly trying not to gag.

Talia, meanwhile, produced a silkworm cocoon from inside her pocket and began to carefully unwind it, producing an impossibly long piece of silk. She walked over to the door and leaned up onto her tiptoes, beginning to pack the silk around the top of the doorframe. Once that was covered, she worked her way down the side, until she reached the bottom and Sumi's layer of well-chewed gum. The cocoon didn't get any smaller until she had less than a foot to go, at which point it seemed to unravel all at once, leaving her with exactly enough silk to stop the gap.

She straightened, turning back to the Lord of the Dead. "Will that do, sir?" she asked.

"Yes," he said, sounding genuinely impressed. "It will."

THE LADY OF THE DEAD was waiting for them in the library. She gasped when she saw Nancy cradled in her husband's arms, not moving. "What happened to her?" she asked.

"The ghosts took her into the void and kept her there as leverage to have their demands fulfilled," the Lord of the Dead said brusquely. "We retrieved her, and their door has been sealed until their strength bleeds away sufficient to let them through the walls. We need to pay more attention to Our statues. This began because one of them died, and his lover couldn't stand the thought of life without him."

"We understand love," said the Lady.

"No one understands love, but We should be empathetic toward it," said the Lord. "We'll do better."

He stretched Nancy out on one of the library tables. She lay there silently, eyes closed, chest rising and falling in a way that was paradoxically more worrying than anything else about her. For her breathing to be that visible—that *normal*—she had to be so deep into unconsciousness that she could no longer keep herself still, no matter what her training told her.

Her body was in command now, and all it cared about was breathing.

"How long was she in the void?" asked the Lady.

"About an hour," said Kade. "I don't understand. We all went into the void, and we're all fine."

"But you didn't *stay* there," she said. "The void . . . it drains the living, given time to do so. Especially if they're not doing anything to fight it."

"Which Nancy wasn't, because you taught her to hold still to get away from her problems," said Sumi, scowling. "Is she going to get better?"

"We can hope so," said the Lord of the Dead. "She's outside the void now, and back where she belongs. We'll bring her pomegranate juice and sugar wafers, and she'll have all the support We can give her as she recovers."

"Thank you," said the Lady. "Thank you for letting her bring you here, and thank you for saving the rest of our statues. They didn't deserve that death."

"How do we go home?" asked Christopher.

"These are My halls, and My Halls," said the Lord of the Dead. "I command them—within reason. I couldn't seal that door without a physical barrier, and I cannot command the stone to turn to fog or anything of the sort. But if I request a door, one will be opened for Me. We will care for Nancy, and you will go."

"What about my moths?" asked Talia.

"Their share of the fruit is still theirs," said the Lady of the Dead. "Send them back to the groves, and I promise we won't harm their caterpillars or seek to drive them from the trees."

Talia moved to the window, murmuring to the moths that accompanied her. She pushed the window open, and they flew out, wings bright against the sky as they fluttered off into the distance. Talia sighed, watching them go, only looking back when Sumi put a hand on her shoulder and squeezed lightly.

"You did a good job," said Sumi. "Your turn will come. There will be other moths."

Talia sighed again and walked with her back to Christopher and Kade, who were watching the Lord of the Dead with sharp, wary eyes.

He put a hand on the door out of the library, pausing a moment before pulling it carefully open to reveal the basement at the school.

Kade looked back at Nancy, motionless on the table, then stepped through. The others followed him, only Talia hesitating.

"I promised the moths I would sing their verses of the Great Song to the rest of the eclipse," she said, looking to the Lord of the Dead. "Can I stay long enough for that?"

The Lord of the Dead paused, saying nothing. The Lady turned and gave him a hard look. After a long moment he sighed and looked away.

"The door will remain for another hour," he said. "You may sing your songs."

"Thank you," said Talia, voice dripping with relief. She left the room then, leaving the Lord and Lady behind.

"The living are so demanding," he said wearily.

The Lady only laughed.

An hour later, Talia returned, leaves in her hair and contentment in her eyes. She walked straight to the door and through. It swung shut behind her, popping like a soap bubble, and she was back in the basement, back in the familiar air of school.

Christopher, sitting on the bed, looked up from his flute practice and smiled. "Sumi said you'd be along. We decided to trust her, because it was better than trying to get back into the Halls of the Dead when we didn't know how. Come on. Let's go tell Miss West you're back."

He slid easily off the bed, heading for the stairs. Talia didn't argue.

She just followed.

15 HOME AGAIN

SIX MONTHS LATER . . .

THE BASEMENT WAS EMPTY when the door appeared on the wall. As soon as it was there, it looked as if it had been there forever, as solid as any other piece of the house. The door swung open, framing a girl with black-and-white hair. She was dressed in a white peplos, and her feet were bare. She began to step over the threshold and stopped, putting a hand on the doorframe as she momentarily closed her eyes.

"Thank you," she whispered. "For everything, thank you. You will always be my home."

The door didn't answer her in any way. After a moment she took her hand away, opened her eyes, and stepped fully out of the doorway. The door closed behind her, disappearing. She didn't look back, only started for the stairs, moving with the smooth, unhurried steps of someone who had seen the beauty in stillness, and was now trying to remember the good grace of motion, the virtue of being an active participant in her own life.

Grasping the bannister tightly, Nancy Whitman began her progress toward the future, looking forward all the way.

ABOUT THE AUTHOR

Beckett Gladney

SEANAN MCGUIRE is the author of the Hugo, Nebula, Alex, and Locus Award–winning Wayward Children series, the October Daye series, the InCryptid series, and other works. She also writes darker fiction as Mira Grant. McGuire lives in Seattle with her cats, a vast collection of creepy dolls, horror movies, and sufficient books to qualify her as a fire hazard. She won the 2010 John W. Campbell Award for Best New Writer, and in 2013 became the first person to appear five times on the same Hugo ballot. In 2022 she managed the same feat, again!